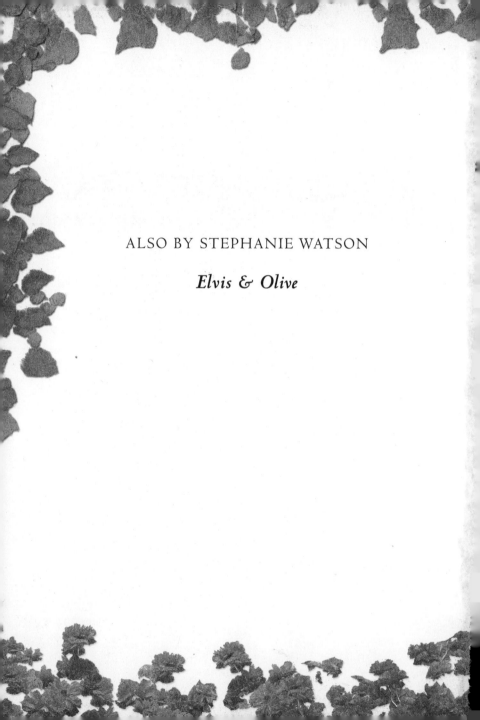

ALSO BY STEPHANIE WATSON

Elvis & Olive

Elvis & Olive
Super Detectives

By
STEPHANIE WATSON

SCHOLASTIC PRESS · NEW YORK

An Imprint of Scholastic Inc.

Library of Congress Cataloging-in-Publication Data

Watson, Stephanie Elaine, 1979–
Elvis & Olive : super detectives / by Stephanie Watson. — 1st ed.
p. cm.
Summary: When best friends Natalie, age ten, and Annie, nine, form a detective
agency to solve neighborhood mysteries, Natalie hopes it will help her win a school
election, while Annie seeks the mother who abandoned her.
ISBN 978-0-545-15148-1 (hardcover)
[1. Best friends — Fiction.   2. Friendship — Fiction.   3. Politics, Practical —
Fiction.   4. Schools — Fiction.   5. Mothers and daughters — Fiction.   6. Foster
home care — Fiction.   7. Mystery
and detective stories.]   I. Title.   II. Title: Elvis and Olive.

PZ7.W3295Elm 2010
[Fic] — dc22
2009026074

10 9 8 7 6 5 4 3 2 1   10 11 12 13 14

Printed in the U.S.A.   23
First edition, July 2010

The text type was set in Centaur Roman.
Book design by Elizabeth B. Parisi

To Mom and Dad

Chapter One

O n the day ten-year-old Natalie Wallis nominated herself for Student Council Secretary, the
bus ride home felt like flying. After two years of shyly
hoping someone would raise a hand to nominate her,
Natalie had raised her own hand. Her fingers shook,
but she did it.

The secretary's job was to run the School Store on
Friday afternoons, and sell pencils and other supplies
at the folding table outside the principal's office. For
Natalie, who adored school supplies as much as she
loved books, being elected Student Council Secretary
would be a dream come true. A dream filled with rows
and rows of new peppery-smelling pencils that had
never written wrong answers. Stacks of soft, bright

erasers that had never touched mistakes. And crisp notebooks, blank with possibility.

Despite her shyness, Natalie had taken charge of her own nomination, and now she was in the running! *Was this a good day or what?* Natalie stuck her hand out the open bus window, giving the soft September air a high five. It high-fived back.

Tall oaks, elms, and maples formed a leafy roof over Natalie's street, making the whole block feel like one big house. After school, Natalie sat on her front steps with her nine-year-old best friend who lived across the street. Annie Beckett was her real name, but Natalie called her Elvis, for short, and because it was her code name. Natalie's code name was Olive.

"Don't think it's just pencils, Elvis," said Natalie. "The School Store has pens that write in four colors, and mini staplers shaped like dogs and cats, and so many fruity erasers, you can smell them halfway down the hall."

"No *way*," Annie said, slapping her hands to her cheeks dramatically. Her fingers were dirt-stained from digging a grave for the squirrel tail she'd found in the street.

"There's glitter glue," Natalie gushed, "and folders in every color of the rainbow." She broke a granola bar in two and handed the bigger half, wrapped in a napkin, to Annie.

Annie tossed the napkin aside and grabbed the bar with her bare, filthy hands — she didn't care about germs. She tapped crumbs off the end as if it were a cigar, then took a big bite. "At Jefferson, we don't have a school store," Annie said. She went to a public school across town from Natalie's private academy. "We have to buy our pencils elsewhere."

"The School Store sells all *kinds* of pencils," Natalie continued. "Glitter, neon, cartoon, camouflage, jumbo, scented, smiley face — even pencils that change color in the heat of your hand. And there's a hole puncher that punches heart-shaped holes!"

"Heart-shaped holes?" Annie faked a faint. "It's *not possible.*"

Natalie rolled her eyes. "Do I make fun of the things you like? Do I tease you when you tell me the plot of every single episode of *The Arthur Milligan Mysteries*?"

"Not yet," said Annie.

"Elvis, Student Council is important to me. Running the School Store has been my number-one dream for two years."

Annie studied Natalie's face carefully. "I will help you achieve that dream, Olive. What's the first step?"

"To prove that I'd make a good public role model, I have to do a Helping Hands project."

"What's that?" Annie pulled two clementine oranges from her coat pocket and handed the larger one to Natalie.

"The project can be anything," Natalie said, "as long as it helps the neighborhood in some way. I can pick up trash or collect cans for a food shelf or —"

"Or open a detective agency," Annie interrupted.

Natalie stopped peeling her clementine. "What does a detective agency have to do with helping our neighbors?"

"We'll solve mysteries for people. I can't think of anything *more* helpful." Annie bit into a fat clementine slice, sending a spray of juice onto the concrete. "And I've wanted to become a detective for a while now."

"Elvis, you know how much trouble we got into this summer by spying on people," Natalie said. "We promised we wouldn't do it anymore."

Annie shook her head. "Detectives are way different from spies. Spies peek through curtains in secret. Detectives solve cases out in the open, for people who want to be helped."

It still sounded like trouble. "I'd feel more comfortable collecting soup cans," said Natalie. "Principal Tangleton is going to evaluate everybody's projects, and she's strict. What if she doesn't like the detective idea?"

Annie stuffed the rest of the clementine into her cheek like a squirrel. "Let's make a deal: We'll have a detective agency for a week. If it doesn't work out, I'll pull the soup-can wagon while you knock on doors. Either way, you'll have a really great Helping Hands project. Okay?"

Natalie pushed the neon orange peels into a neat pile on the stoop. "Okay."

"Yay!" Annie cried. "Let's get our detective costumes."

Annie ran home to grab what would become her official detective outfit — a blue choir robe she had found in the alley during their summer of spying. Meanwhile, Natalie hurried up to her bedroom to change out of her private-school uniform and grab her pink cowboy boots — the ones she'd discovered in the same alley. The boots, meant to be Natalie's detective costume, had fit better a couple of months ago. Now they pinched a little. Natalie stepped out the porch door, her gaze fixed on the scuffed toes. Out of the corner of her eye, she saw Annie standing on the sidewalk in her dark robe.

"My feet grew," Natalie announced.

"Uh . . . they did?" Steven Redding looked up from the big black trash bag he was holding.

"Oh! I thought you were Annie," Natalie said, her face starting to burn.

For three years, Natalie had had a secret crush on twelve-year-old Steven Redding, who lived on her block. He had the kind of face that made your heart turn to hot gravy when you looked at it. His sweet brown eyes, rimmed with long lashes, were kind, yet mischievous. The crescent-moon scar high on his left cheekbone gave him an air of mystery. But his smile was the thing that really killed Natalie. It crept up higher on one side, which made Steven's mouth seem like it was making an inside joke with you.

Steven went to Natalie's school and lived just a handful of houses away from her. But he might have been miles away for all the good it did Natalie. During the summer, when her secret crush had come out, Steven told Natalie that he liked her, too — but only as a friend. There was no reason to think he might change his mind. Still, Natalie could not help hoping, though she tried to hide it.

"So," said Natalie, as casually as she could, "what are you up to?"

Steven held up a dirty leaf. "I'm trying to decide if this counts as garbage or just nature."

"Nature."

"Shoot." Steven let the leaf flutter to the sidewalk. "I need to fill this whole trash bag before dinner."

"Why?" asked Natalie.

"I have to do a Helping Hands project, and picking up our neighbors' garbage is part of it."

"Helping Hands? You're running for Student Council?" Natalie's heart started skipping rope.

"Unfortunately," Steven said with a sigh. "It's all because of the prank with the Bechrachs and the cars."

During the summer, Steven had taken part in a scheme to wash windshields at stoplights to make a few bucks. It was Tom Bechrach's idea, and he was the one who dented a red convertible with a hammer when the driver didn't pay up. It wasn't Steven's fault, except that he picked the wrong day to hang out with the Bechrachs.

"I'm still in trouble with my parents about that," Steven said. "My dad wants me to prove I can be more responsible." He examined a broken branch before stuffing it into the trash bag. "It was either work weekends at my mom's aerobics studio or run for Student Council."

"I'm running, too," said Natalie. *We are running side by side. Hand in hand.*

"Oh, cool," said Steven. "What's your Helping Hands gig?"

"I'm . . . a detective." She pointed stupidly at her cowboy boots.

Before she had a chance to explain what cowboy boots had to do with it, and that the whole thing was Annie's idea, their conversation was cut short by the shrill scream of a whistle. Noah Redding, Steven's younger brother, jogged toward them. His stiff blue jeans made a *fip-fip-fip* sound as the inseams rubbed together.

Every day, no matter the weather, Noah wore the

same pair of jeans. Despite getting so much use, they were always extra-dark blue and so starchy Noah could barely bend his knees as he ran.

"Come on, criminal!" Noah shouted. "Let me see you work that trash bag."

Steven dropped the bag to the sidewalk. "Seriously, Noah, you need to stop." He turned to Natalie. "In case I forget that I'm being punished, I have my own personal policeman to remind me."

Noah was ten — Natalie's age — but he didn't act like it. He tortured bugs, pulling off their wings and legs for fun. He was nasty to people, too, banning everyone from sitting with him on the school bus. For years, he had been in Natalie's class at Newton Academy. But luckily, he was in a different fifth-grade class this year.

Noah tooted his whistle at Steven. "Fill that bag."

"Careful, top cop," Steven said. "This bag is plenty big for you *and* your whistle."

"Okay, okay. But I'm watching you. And you."

Noah glared at Natalie, who was picking up a smashed taco wrapper from the gutter.

"I'm just helping," she said.

"No helping allowed," said Noah. "Criminals should carry out their sentences alone."

"So leave me alone then!" Steven whip-snapped the trash bag at his brother, who took off running. The sound of Noah's jeans rubbing together faded as he got farther away. *Fip-fip-fip-fip-fip.*

"It's going to take me all night to fill this bag," Steven said.

"There's always trash in the alley," Natalie said. "Check there."

"Oh, good call." Steven held out his fist for some sort of handshake Natalie didn't understand. Hesitantly, she offered her fist. Steven lightly knocked it with his knuckles before opening his hand into a starburst. "See ya, Detective," he said.

Before cutting through the yard into the alley, he smiled his perfectly crooked, inside-joke smile at her.

Natalie felt the world expand and stretch with possibility, like a giant rubber band.

Becoming Student Council Secretary would be fantastic. But if Steven was elected to Student Council, too? That was miles beyond her wildest hopes. They'd both attend Council meetings on Mondays after school, and maybe get a ride home together from a teacher. What if Steven was running for treasurer? That would mean he'd sit beside Natalie at the School Store table on Fridays, collecting a quarter in the metal money box for every pencil she sold. They would stand next to each other in the Student Council yearbook picture, and decades from now Natalie would show it to people and say, "This is the day Steven stopped seeing me as only a friend."

Annie dashed out her porch door and down the concrete steps, the hem of her choir robe billowing beneath her.

"Sorry I took so long. I had to ask Grandma Hatch where she stashed my robe." Annie rolled up the droopy sleeves. "Who should we help first?"

"Wait," Natalie said. "If we're really going to be detectives, we have to do it right. Let's do some research first."

Annie raised one eyebrow. "Research?"

"Yeah, to learn some techniques. Oooh! I know: Let's check out detective novels from the library. I'll read some and you read some, and we'll copy what the characters do."

Annie, who didn't think much of reading, snorted. "Books aren't the only place detectives live, you know. They're also on TV. And in case you forgot, the secretary from *The Arthur Milligan Mysteries* is our neighbor."

Virginia Brooks lived a few houses down from Annie. Many years before Natalie and Annie were born, she had starred in *The Arthur Milligan Mysteries*, a hit TV show. Ms. Brooks had the role of Agent Milligan's smart and sassy assistant, Miss Dimesworth.

Now the show played in reruns on Channel 12, and Natalie had watched a few episodes with Annie, because it was Annie's favorite show of all time. Knowing how much TV Annie had watched in her life, that was saying something. And Natalie had to admit: The episodes she had seen were pretty okay.

"We could ask Virginia for some tips," said Annie.

"Yeah," said Natalie. "If we can convince her to open the door."

Chapter Two

Virginia Brooks cracked open her front door just enough to reveal her thin, painted lips.

"I don't want to buy any cookies or wrapping paper or Christmas wreaths or firewood. Good-bye," she whispered, and creaked the door closed.

Ms. Brooks never came outside. She never spoke to the neighbors. Annie said it was because she was sad she wasn't on TV anymore.

"We're not selling anything," Natalie called through the mail slot.

"Oh, petition people, are you? I don't sign petitions. I don't want any of your pamphlets, either."

"No," Annie said. "We want to ask you about *The Arthur Milligan Mysteries*."

Slowly the door opened, a little wider this time. Ms. Brooks's drawn-on eyebrows lifted hopefully. "An interview? Nobody's asked for an interview in years."

"Yes," Annie said. "An interview with Miss Dimesworth."

Clutching the neck of her faded silk kimono closed, Ms. Brooks invited the girls in. She led them back to the living room, which was clearly a shrine to the golden years of *The Arthur Milligan Mysteries*.

Hanging on the wall were posters as tall as Natalie of seasons one, two, and three of the show. A mannequin in the corner wore a brown bouffant wig and a beige trench coat à la Miss Dimesworth, played by Ms. Virginia Brooks. Two golden trophies sat atop the fireplace mantel, next to a Barbie-sized Miss Dimesworth doll.

Annie grabbed the doll and yanked the cord in its back.

"The answer is to ask more questions!" the doll squeaked.

"Don't touch that!" Ms. Brooks cried. "It's a collector's item."

"Sorry." Annie carefully put the doll back on its metal stand and glanced around. "Wow. I can't believe I'm in *Miss Dimesworth's* house."

Ms. Brooks's face softened. "Will you sit down?"

Natalie and Annie settled on the chintz couch, next to a life-size cardboard cutout of Agent Milligan. He wore a sly grin and an actual felt detective hat. Annie shook his cardboard hand.

Natalie opened her notebook. "Ms. Brooks, we're brand-new detectives, and we need some tips from an expert. Mind if we ask you some questions?"

Ms. Brooks looked pleased. "Go right ahead."

"Question one," said Natalie. "What are the tools that a detective needs?"

Ms. Brooks crossed one knee gracefully over the other. "Well, you're already using the most important tool."

Natalie stopped writing. "A pencil?"

"No," said Ms. Brooks, "although pencils do come in handy. I'm talking about *questions*."

"Questions?" Annie said. "What about them?"

"*You're* using them, too! You're a natural detective."

"Miss Dimesworth called me a natural," Annie said, hugging herself. "Am I dreaming?"

"My, look at you go with those questions!" Ms. Brooks said. She pulled a boxed set of *The Arthur Milligan Mysteries* from the TV cabinet. "Let's watch an episode to see what else you can learn."

"Miss Dimesworth, this case is cold." Agent Milligan took a noisy slurp of coffee. "Mr. Peabiddy has no idea where the money is — you could see it plainly on his face in the interrogation."

Miss Dimesworth patted her bouffant hairdo. "I wouldn't know, Arthur. I was watching Mrs. Peabiddy. She looked as guilty as a dog with doughnut dust on its whiskers."

"Hmm . . . Mrs. Peabiddy. That could be,"

said Agent Milligan, stroking his mustache. "Now what?"

Miss Dimesworth put one hand on her hip. "The answer is to ask more questions."

After Miss Dimesworth and Agent Milligan solved the mystery of the missing Peabiddy fortune, the credits rolled. Annie bounced on the couch cushions and sang along with the closing theme song. *"If Milligan can't solve it, Dimesworth DOES!"*

Natalie flipped back a few pages in her notebook. "Let's review what we learned."

"Good detective teams pace around a lot. They say catchphrases." Annie listed off her fingers. "They stroke their mustaches, if they have them."

"Good detectives also ask a lot of questions and listen closely for the answers," Natalie read from her notes. "They think of everything as a potential clue. And if they ever get stuck, they ask more questions."

"You got it," said Ms. Brooks.

Annie rubbed her upper lip. "What I wouldn't give for a mustache."

"You know, the actor who played Agent Milligan didn't have a real mustache. He wore a false one." Ms. Brooks pointed to a glass display case by the window.

"Really?" Annie leaped from the couch and gaped at the thick brown mustache under the glass.

"It's made of human hair," said Ms. Brooks.

"Wowie," Annie said. "Real human hair. I want one."

"Thanks for all your help, Ms. Brooks," Natalie tugged the back of Annie's choir robe. "Elvis, let go of the case."

Annie's fingers squeaked as she dragged them longingly across the glass. She spun to face Ms. Brooks. "Will you put on the costume for us?"

Ms. Brooks looked horrified. "I *never* put on the costume. Dust it, yes. Wear it, no."

"Why not?" Annie asked.

Ms. Brooks let her gaze drift down to the carpet like a stone sinking underwater. "I'm not Miss Dimesworth anymore," she said. "Those were good times, but they're over now."

"Maybe the good times would come back if you tried on the costume," Natalie suggested.

Ms. Brooks shook her head stiffly. "No."

"Will you at least say the line?" Annie begged. "Just once?"

Judging by Ms. Brooks's tightly pursed lips, Natalie was sure she wouldn't do it. But after a deep sigh, Ms. Virginia Brooks straightened her back. She put a hand on her hip and raised one eyebrow. "The answer," she said, "is to ask more questions."

The late-afternoon sun was warm, but the shadowy spots held the cool tang of fall. A brisk wind blew through the neighborhood's trees, making the leaves quiver like little hands waving good-bye to summer.

"Now that we're all trained up, you pick who we help first," Annie said.

"Why do I have to pick?"

"As a leader on Student Council," Annie explained, "you'll need to make important decisions. This Helping Hands stuff is practice."

"That's true," said Natalie. "Let's see." She looked up and down the street, at the old houses with their front porches and pointy roofs. She imagined her neighbors moving around inside their houses. Then she imagined mysteries moving around inside the neighbors, trying to find a way out.

After a minute, Natalie nodded toward the yellow house on the corner, the one right across the street from her own house. "Let's see if Ms. Hatch wants a helping hand."

"Good idea, Olive."

Ms. Hatch was Annie's new foster parent, though since she was sixty-nine years old, she was more of a foster grandparent. Annie had lived with her only a couple of weeks, since the end of August.

The girls bounded up the steps, and Annie rang the bell. It took a minute for a stout woman with a high, gray ponytail to come to the door. She was wiping her wet hands on a clay-stained apron.

"Why, Annie, you don't need to ring the bell," said the woman. "This is your home now, too. Just come in."

"I rang because we're on *official business*." Annie rocked back and forth on her heels.

"*Oh,*" Ms. Hatch said with a nod of understanding. "Then let's try this again."

Ms. Hatch, unlike most adults, knew when to play along. She hustled back into the house and shut the door. Annie rang the bell again. Ms. Hatch reappeared in the doorway. "Hello?" she said and looked at the girls searchingly, as if she did not know them. "Can I . . . help you?"

Annie stepped forward. "A better question is if *we* can help *you*," she said. "My name is Elvis. This is Olive. And together, we are the E & O Detective Agency. We solve mysteries. Got any?"

"It's free," Natalie added.

"Well . . ." Ms. Hatch glanced down at her feet. The left foot wore a black beaded slipper. The right foot, a red rubber flip-flop. "Earlier today, I was throwing a vase on my potter's wheel. I was kicking the wheel hard to make it go fast. Perhaps I kicked a little *too* hard, because my flip-flop went flying!" She traced an arc in the air. "I couldn't find it anywhere. So I put on this slipper and went back to work."

Annie studied Ms. Hatch's feet and nodded. "We'll find your flip-flop, ma'am. No problem."

Chapter Three

The best part about Ms. Hatch's house was the pottery studio in the first-floor sunroom. It smelled of wet clay mixed with perfumed candles, and the dusty radio in the corner was always playing jazz. A clay-spattered potter's wheel sat in the middle of the room like a throne. Tall wooden shelves lined the walls with pots and vases of all shapes and sizes. Most of the pieces were some shade of purple, and all of them were lopsided.

Ms. Hatch's hands weren't as steady on the potter's wheel as they once had been. But shaky hands weren't something that could stop Ms. Hatch. She loved making pots and vases, crooked or not. Annie and

Natalie had helped Ms. Hatch realize that people liked her pottery enough to buy it, and now she sold it at three different gift shops in town.

"So you were working here," Natalie said, resting a hand on the motionless potter's wheel. "You were kicking the pedal, and then your sandal flew off. Right?"

"It flew that way," Ms. Hatch said. She pointed to a row of violet-colored vases as high as Natalie's waist — meant to be umbrella stands, maybe. "That's the last I saw of it."

"Perhaps it was *stolen*," said Annie. She stroked an imaginary mustache.

"No, I don't think so." Ms. Hatch scratched the back of her hand, where a clay smear had hardened to a crust.

"Definitely stolen," Annie said, pacing the room with heavy steps. "Someone walked in here and took the sandal without you even noticing. A professional, obviously."

While Annie ranted, Natalie reached into the dark mouth of one of the tall vases against the wall. Empty.

She tried the next one over, and her fingers curled around a rubbery strap. "I found it," she said, holding up the clay-encrusted flip-flop.

"Oh!" Ms. Hatch exclaimed. "Wonderful!"

Natalie stuck her arm back into the vase. "There's something else in here." She withdrew a dusty paintbrush.

"My size-two brush — I've been looking for that!" Ms. Hatch said, accepting both lost things from Natalie.

"Good work!" Annie said, giving Natalie a dusty clap on the back.

Ms. Hatch shook Natalie's hand in a very official way. Then she shook Annie's hand before pulling her into a strong hug.

"You girls are fine detectives. I will recommend your services highly."

"This case was solved one-hundred percent by Olive," Annie said.

Natalie shrugged. "I just asked simple questions and used common sense."

"As all great detectives do," said Ms. Hatch. "Now,

27

who's hungry for cookies? I baked too many again. Will you help some of them go missing?"

In Ms. Hatch's kitchen, Natalie politely chose one of the rose-shaped cookies. Annie took a stack.

"Are you convinced yet?" Annie asked. "Being a detective is helpful."

"And it's fun," Natalie admitted.

"Yes, it is," Annie said. She waited until Ms. Hatch had left the kitchen, then said, "To make our detective agency official, let's say a pledge in our headquarters."

Their club headquarters was the crawl space under the porch of the house next to Ms. Hatch's. Until the end of August, Annie had lived in that run-down house with her uncle Ralph and his girlfriend Charla. But when Charla wanted to get married and told Ralph it was her or Annie, Ralph picked his girlfriend. That's when Ms. Hatch invited Annie to live with her, in her house on the corner, and became her foster grandparent.

"We can't use the headquarters," Natalie said. "It's not your house anymore."

"So? No one else has moved in yet." Before Natalie could protest again, Annie had elbowed open the kitchen door, then the back gate. Her hands full of cookies, she headed for the house next door.

Annie's two houses stood side by side on the block, but they had totally different faces. Ms. Hatch's house had wide, bright-eyed windows and a smile made of marigold-filled window boxes. Annie's old house next door looked like it had been in a fight — and lost. One of the front windows was broken, and the bruise-colored siding was warping away from the house. Like an unshaven beard, the lawn was tangled with every type of prickly weed. The dented screen door had fallen off the porch when Ralph and Charla were moving out, and no one had fixed it. The gaping doorway was an endless, silent howl.

Annie waded across the overgrown lawn and kneeled at the spot in the porch foundation where the wooden boards had rotted away. This shoulder-width hole was the entrance to the club headquarters. Annie crawled through it.

"*Elvis*," Natalie said.

"Come on, Olive." Annie's voice echoed from the dark hole. "We won't get in trouble." Natalie looked around to make sure no one was watching. On her hands and knees, she inched inside.

Annie dug out their candle and matches from the wooden crate in the corner. Rasping a match against its box, she transferred the bright flame to the candle-wick. The flickering light revealed the short wooden walls and dirt floor of their old hideout. Natalie tugged the dusty green army blanket from the crate and spread it on the floor, so they wouldn't have to sit on the dirt. Once they were settled, Natalie pulled Ms. Hatch's rose cookie from her pocket and snapped off a petal.

"Ms. Hatch is a good baker," Natalie said. "And she's so nice. Do you like living with her?"

"Yeah," Annie said. "She's really sweet. When my mom comes back, I'll visit Grandma Hatch all the time."

Natalie nearly choked on her cookie. *Annie's mom was coming back?*

A year and a half ago, Annie's mom had left Annie alone at their apartment in Resselville, one town over, saying she was going to buy a gallon of ice cream at the corner convenience store. She never came home. No one knew where she went or where she was now. Not her brother, Ralph, who eventually became Annie's foster parent. Not Ms. Hatch, who took Annie in after Ralph left town himself. No one knew.

When Natalie stopped coughing on cookie crumbs, she asked, "When will your mom be back?"

"I don't know exactly *when*," Annie said. "I have to find her first. That's why I became a detective."

"Oh," Natalie said. Now Annie's eagerness to open a detective agency made sense. Natalie knew how much Annie missed her mom — it was a deep, dark hole inside her. But was trying to find her a good idea? It wouldn't be easy. She could be anywhere. Plus, she had run away on purpose, right? So even if Annie did find her mom, what if her mom didn't want to come back?

There were a lot of unanswered questions. But

Natalie knew one thing for sure: If her own mom were somewhere out there, Natalie would need to look for her, too. Even if the search seemed hopeless.

With her fingertip, Annie drew an airplane in the dirt floor. She gave it long, smooth wings and a sharp tail. "You'll help me look for her, right?"

Natalie said, "I will."

"Thanks, Olive." Annie swept away the dust airplane with her shoe. "Let's do the pledge now. Hold your hand over the swear bird."

Annie hovered her hand over the spot where she had once buried a dead baby bird. Natalie perched her hand on top of Annie's.

"As a detective for the E & O Detective Agency," said Annie, "I solemnly swear to help our neighbors solve their mysteries."

"But only if they want us to," Natalie added.

"And I swear," said Annie, "to do what it takes to get Olive elected for Student Council Secretary, because she is my best friend and she deserves it."

"And I swear to help Elvis look for her mom," Natalie said, "and be her best friend for all time."

"Amen!" Annie cried, and spit on the candle flame to officially end the meeting.

At bedtime, as an autumn storm raged just outside her window, Natalie climbed under her covers and clicked on her flashlight. She pointed the beam at the headboard of her bed.

Ever since Natalie could remember, the headboard had been missing a tiny chip of paint. The lost chip formed the perfect profile of a woman with a gracefully pointy nose and long hair. She faced sideways because, Natalie imagined, she wanted to leave her ear available to hear Natalie's confessions. Natalie often told the paint-chip lady secrets, because she had all the time in the world to listen and would never tell.

Thunder rattled the windowpane while Natalie handed confessions over to the paint-chip lady one by one, as if emptying her pockets.

I still like Steven even though I'm trying not to.

I wish being a leader came as easily to me as it does to Annie.

There was one more secret to tell, and it was heavy. Natalie was glad to hand it over.

I promised to help Annie find her mom, Natalie whispered. *But I don't think she will ever come back. Should I tell Annie the truth, or pretend I believe? What would a good friend do?*

Lightning winked between the curtains. The paint-chip lady stared silently at the wall. That was the one problem with a friend made of missing paint — she never gave any answers. Natalie would have to discover the answers for herself.

Chapter Four

The next day, Saturday, Natalie spent her one daily hour of TV time on a PBS documentary about bees. But instead of paying attention to the show, Natalie daydreamed about Student Council. And Steven, of course.

It's two-thirty on a Friday afternoon. Natalie, Student Council Secretary, gets the School Store supplies from the locked janitor's office with the key they gave to her on a special keychain. She carries the supplies to the table at the end of the main hallway. There, she arranges the pencils, erasers, and folders, first according to color, then alphabetically. At precisely two forty-five, Steven, Student Council Treasurer, shows up with the metal money box.

"Hey, partner," he says.

Together, they open the School Store for business. Natalie tucks purchases into crisp paper bags, and Steven collects the money in a perfectly synchronized dance. When the rush of customers slows, Steven turns to her.

"What's your favorite pencil on this table?" he asks.

Natalie pauses, as if unsure, as if she hasn't imagined this question a thousand times before. "Hmm. I guess . . . the pink one with glitter stars."

Steven pulls a shiny quarter from his back pocket. He flips it into the metal money box with a clink.

"The pencil is yours." He smiles and winks at Natalie. Yes, he winks!

"Thank you," Natalie says. "What's your favorite pencil?"

"I've been waiting my whole life for someone to ask me that," Steven says. "The mechanical one."

"With the spare box of leads?"

Steven nods. Natalie unzips her backpack and fishes two quarters from the front pocket. She slides them across the table to Steven.

"Take the pencil and the leads."

"No, it's too much," Steven protests.

"Please," Natalie insists.

Steven rolls the ends of the mechanical pencil between his fingers. "Okay. But I'll never be able to do another algebra problem without thinking of you, Natalie. Natalie."

"NATALIE." Ricky Wallis, Natalie's six-year-old brother, stood in front of the TV with a board-game box pressed to his hip bones. "Will you play a game with me?"

"I'm watching my show," said Natalie.

"No you're not. You're staring at a pencil."

Natalie set down the pencil she hadn't realized she was holding. The daydream was over. "Okay. One game."

Natalie usually couldn't stand Chutes and Ladders — it was depressing to land on the biggest slide. But today, she was so happy and hopeful about Student Council, and about Steven, that she sat on the floor and helped Ricky set up the board. For once, Natalie didn't mind playing.

Light from the headquarters candle glinted off the scissor blades Annie held over her head. She grabbed a hunk of white-blond hair near her neck and snipped it off.

"Elvis, I'm going to say it one last time," Natalie said. "You should *not* cut your own hair."

"You think it stays this short on its own?" Annie pruned her spiky bangs. "I've been cutting it myself since I was seven. Hand me the tape."

Natalie reluctantly passed Annie a roll of tape from her backpack. "If you gave yourself a bald spot, good luck taping the hair back on."

Annie laughed. "It's not for that." She ripped a short strip of tape from the roll. Holding the strip at both ends, Annie dipped it into the pile of clippings on the army blanket. Now the tape was covered in hair, except for the far edges. These, Annie used to stick her homemade mustache to her top lip. She checked out her reflection in the mirrored scissor blades. "Made of real human hair, just like Agent Milligan's."

"It looks pretty cool," Natalie admitted. "It matches your head hair."

"Oh, do you want one?" Annie snickered the scissor

blades open and closed, and scooted toward Natalie. "Your hair is so long, you can make one of those big twirly mustaches. Lucky!"

Natalie grabbed her braids and backed against the wall. "No way are you cutting my hair," she said. "Elvis, seriously. Don't we have some detective work to do?"

"Yes." Annie set the scissors aside. "Are you ready to find out where my mom is?"

"Okay," Natalie said. "But how?"

Annie reached into her back pocket and withdrew a dingy gold coin, bigger than a quarter. It was stamped with the face of a clown on the front side, a circus tent on the back, and the words "Resselville Arcade. No cash value."

Annie had two of these coins, and Natalie knew how special they were to her. Not long before Annie's mom had run off, she'd taken Annie to the Resselville Arcade. They stayed there all day playing Skee-Ball, Annie had said. There were two game tokens left at closing time, and Annie's mom promised they would go back and spend them soon. But before that could happen, Annie's mom had left for good.

"You think your mom's at the Resselville Arcade?" Natalie asked. "My parents probably won't let me go there." Resselville, especially the area where Annie used to live, was a rough place.

"We're not going anywhere," Annie said. "The answers will come to us. Watch."

She held the coin in her open palm.

"Is my mom in Pennsylvania?" Annie asked. She tossed the coin in the air, caught it, and slapped it onto the back of her hand. The side of the coin with the big-top tent was face-up. "Circus tent. That means no."

"You're asking the *coin* questions?"

Annie nodded. "I ask a yes or no question and flip the coin. If the clown face comes up, that means yes. Circus tent is no."

"Elvis," Natalie said, "when Ms. Brooks told us that good detectives ask questions, I don't think this is what she had in mind."

"Maybe not," Annie said. "But the coin works — I just tested it. See, I already knew my mom isn't in Pennsylvania. I only asked that question to make sure the coin tells the truth."

"How do you know she's not in Pennsylvania?"

Annie ran her fingernail along the ridged edge of the coin. "She got in trouble there once," she said. "We can't ever go back."

"What kind of trouble?"

Instead of answering Natalie's question, Annie closed her eyes again. "Is my mom in Oregon?" She flipped the coin and caught it. "Circus tent. Nope."

"Wait. Back up. I want to know more about Pennsylvania."

Annie shook the coin at Natalie. "Listen! My mom's not in Oregon. This is big news."

"What do you mean?" Natalie asked.

"I thought she might've gone back to her parents' house, even though they're both dead," Annie said. "She always talked about a tree in her old backyard that grew gold cherries so sweet they stung your teeth. She promised we'd go there one day and eat them until our teeth ached."

Annie squeezed the coin, as if trying to wring water from it. "She has to come back, so we can do all the things she promised. I *have* to find her."

Natalie was confused. Annie was desperate to find her mom. So why wasn't she conducting a real investigation? Real detectives don't flip coins to solve their cases. Like Miss Dimesworth, they ask tough questions until they discover the truth.

Again and again, Annie flipped the arcade coin off her thumb, where it flashed and spun head over tails in the candlelight. She asked the coin about Disneyland and New York and other glamorous places her mom might be, and the coin said no, no, no.

Natalie thought about how, just like the coin, Annie had two sides, too. There was the side she let Natalie see. The clown. Then, there was a part of herself she hid from everyone, which Natalie could only sense, not see. The circus tent, with its closed door flaps. Natalie sensed that Annie was hiding something now — something to do with her mom. But what?

"Elvis," Natalie said, "you know you can tell me anything. Anything at all."

Annie slowly slipped the arcade token into her pocket. She blinked a few too many times.

"What are you thinking?" Natalie asked.

Annie looked up with a sudden smile. "I'm thinking," she said brightly, "that I'm starving for an apple from Albert's tree."

Albert Castle lived by himself in one of the tallest houses on the block, which made sense because he was the tallest person Natalie had ever met. When he answered Natalie's knock, his head grazed the top of the door frame. A honey-colored guitar hung from a strap over his shoulder.

"*Hel-lo*," Albert sang, strumming the guitar strings.

"Hi, Albert," said Natalie. "Can we pick two apples?"

"Taaake as ma-ny as you waaaant."

"Have you given up talking for singing?" asked Annie.

"Close," said Albert. "I've given up investment banking for songwriting. It's what I've always wanted to do."

"Elvis and I have a new career, too," said Natalie. "We started a detective agency."

"Ah," said Albert. "Is that what the mustache is for?" He pointed to Annie's top lip.

"Yep." Annie smoothed the edges of the tape, which were starting to curl. "It's made of real human hair."

"Do you have any mysteries you need us to solve?" asked Natalie.

Albert plucked the thickest guitar string thoughtfully. It made a low, serious sound. "It's a mystery to me how to write a good song. I'm waiting for ideas, but none have come yet."

"Oh, ideas are easy," Annie said. She leaned against the metal railing. "What do you care about most in the world?"

Albert tilted his head from side to side, as if debating whether or not to say it. "Donna."

"What do you like best about Donna?" Annie asked.

Albert paused. "Her laugh?"

"'Donna's Laugh.' There's the title of your first song."

Albert slid his left hand down the neck of the guitar and up again, giving the string he plucked a swoopy sound. *"Ha! Your laugh hops high like popcorn, Donna."*

"That's catchy," said Natalie.

"Hee! Your laugh swings free like monkeys, Donna."

Annie did a little dance to the brand-new song. "Mystery solved."

"Ho! Your laugh rolls round like doughnuts, Donna." Without taking his eyes from the strings, Albert nodded his thanks and retreated into his house.

Annie pointed at the apple tree, at two giant pieces of fruit hanging near the top. "Those two are ours," Annie said. "I'm going to get them."

Natalie squinted up at the apples. "Okay, but don't hurt yourself."

Annie stripped off her windbreaker and tossed it on the lawn. She jumped up and caught the lowest branch, then swung her feet onto it. She hung upside down and looked at Natalie.

"How come you're not wearing your cowboy boots anymore?" Annie asked.

"I outgrew them. They pinch my pinky toes."

"No boots, no mustache, no costume. There's nothing detective-y about you at all," Annie said.

Natalie shrugged. "I like wearing my own clothes. It's a break from my school uniform."

"What you need is a catchphrase. Oops!" Annie's right knee slipped from the tree, but she caught the bough with both hands.

"For the love of dogs!" Natalie cried. She wished Annie would be more careful.

"That's a *perfect* catchphrase, Olive!" Annie said, climbing higher in the tree.

Natalie held her arms out, in case Annie slipped again. "What's *your* catchphrase?"

"I don't need one," Annie said proudly from her perch. "I have a mustache."

TWEET! *Fip-fip-fip.*

Noah Redding hurried toward the apple tree and spat out his whistle. "Get down from the tree. Now!"

Annie peered through the leafy branches. "Which tree?"

"You're breaking a law!"

"Says who?" Annie asked.

"Me. I'm the sheriff and president of the Law Club. I make the laws of this neighborhood." Noah got up in Natalie's face with a whisper. "That's right. You're not the only one who can have clubs around here."

"Who else is in your club?" asked Natalie. "Or is it just you?"

Noah scowled. "Of course it's not just me."

"Then who else?"

"I'm not going to tell you."

"That's secret code for 'no one'!" Annie shouted from the top branch.

"TICKET!" Noah roared. He wrenched a tiny pink notepad from his incredibly stiff back pocket. He scribbled on it with great fury and thrust the ticket at Natalie. "Give this to your *friend*."

"Noah," Annie called out, "how can you give me a ticket? I thought you loved me. You said so at the end of the summer." She clutched a leafy branch to her chest dramatically.

Noah shoved the notepad back into his pocket, which considering the tightness of his jeans, took a few tries. "That was before I knew you were a criminal."

"What's Annie supposed to do with this?" Natalie waved the pink slip.

"Doy and *duh*. She's supposed to keep it as a warning. Whoever gets three tickets goes to jail."

Natalie crossed her arms. "What jail?"

"Law Club jail. It's going to be nasty." Noah raised a menacing finger. "There will be rats."

Down the block, a lawn mower cleared its throat

to start, then hummed. Steven Redding plodded behind it.

"Elvis, pick an extra apple for me," Natalie said. "I'm going to give it to Steven."

"My brother doesn't like you, you know," Noah said.

Annie tossed two apples down to Natalie.

"Doy and *duh*, Noah," Natalie said. "He's just a friend."

As Natalie walked toward the hum of the lawn mower, an apple in each hand, she thought, *Steven is just a friend for now. But when we are on Student Council together, all that will change.*

Chapter Five

"HOLD ON A SECOND." Steven shut off the lawn mower. "Now I can hear you. What's up?"

Natalie handed him one of the apples from Albert's tree. "I brought you this."

"That is one big apple," Steven said. "Thanks."

"You're welcome," Natalie said shyly. She dug her fingernail into the skin of her own apple, tattooing it with half moons. "Are you done with garbage duty?"

"Yeah," Steven said. "But now I have to mow everyone's grass before the leaves fall. This Helping Hands business is never-ending."

One house over, the side door swung open. A

gorgeous teenage girl with long blond hair clip-clopped out in high heels. Trina George was fourteen and in eighth grade — the highest grade — at Natalie's school, Newton Academy. At the start of the new school year, she had been in a TV commercial for a shoe store. She smiled winningly at the camera and said, "Fall boots are on sale, too!" Her part was only two seconds long, but those two seconds were enough to make Steven Redding, Trina's next-door neighbor, fall even more deeply in love with her than he already was.

"Hey, Trina," Steven called out to her. "Do you have a modeling job today?"

"Audition." Trina tossed her purse into the back seat of a car parked at the curb. She pulled a compact mirror from her pocket and checked her eye makeup. "It's for a TV movie."

"Wow. A movie," Steven said.

Natalie wished that Steven would look at her the way he was looking at Trina. Steven's eyes seemed to wish something, too, but it had nothing to do with Natalie. Trina, as usual, only had eyes for Trina. She smiled at herself in the mirror, then snapped the compact closed.

"Dad!" Trina screamed at her house. "Let's go!"

"I heard you're running for president," Steven said.

Trina rolled her eyes. "Like, ten of my friends nominated me, so I couldn't say no. Here, have a button." She walked onto Steven's lawn and handed him a button with her picture on it. It said:

Trina George for President
The answer to your prayers

It wasn't like the paper buttons everyone else made — that Natalie was planning on making. Trina's button was professionally made of metal, and her laminated photo looked like something out of a teen magazine. Trina didn't offer Natalie a button, or even acknowledge that she was there, but that was nothing unusual. Trina wasn't ever nice to Natalie, especially not since the summer.

Last summer, Natalie and Annie had spied on

Trina and discovered that she liked to steal jewelry and perfume. Natalie meant to keep it a secret, but Trina's parents found out anyway, and Trina was grounded from the mall for a month. Natalie and Annie had apologized, but Trina seemed determined never to forgive them, or forget.

"Sweet. Thanks," Steven said as he pinned the button to his shirt.

If Trina was elected President — and she would be because she was so popular — the Student Council meetings would be no fun. Not with Trina bossing everyone around. Natalie wished eighth graders weren't allowed to run for Student Council. But the rule was that anyone in any grade could run for any position. What a dumb rule.

"My dad is such an idiot," Trina said. "I'm going to be a million years late to my audition." While she waited for her dad to appear, Trina told Steven how she couldn't wait to add "President" to her acting resume, to impress movie directors.

Natalie tuned out Trina's chatter and watched the long shadows the late-afternoon sun was casting on the grass. Steven stood a foot away from Natalie, but their shadows stood closer, almost holding hands. Natalie moved her shadow hand a centimeter nearer to Steven's hand. Then another centimeter. Closer, closer, almost — until her real knuckles unexpectedly brushed Steven's. Natalie jerked her hand into her sweatshirt pocket.

"You're running for secretary, right?" Trina asked.

Natalie glanced up. Trina, talking to her? This was new. But no — she wasn't even looking at Natalie. The question was for Steven.

"Yeah," Steven said. "But it's just to make my parents happy. I don't actually want to win. The person to vote for is Natalie."

Wait. What? Steven was running for secretary, same as Natalie? In an instant, Natalie's dream vanished, as if rubbed out by an eraser. Now, no matter who won, there was no way Natalie and Steven could be on Student Council together. No selling pencils side by side at the School Store. No yearbook picture with Steven, no after-school Council meetings with Steven, and no rides home with him, either. Nothing, nothing!

Trina's dad shuffled wearily out the side door. Without saying good-bye, the future president of Student Council hurried to the car at the curb.

"I thought you were running for treasurer," Natalie said to Steven when they were alone. She'd heard that Clara Winkle, a fourth grader, was running against her, and had assumed that was it. She hadn't checked the official list of candidates posted outside the principal's office to make sure.

"Nope. I'm up for secretary. But don't worry." Steven started up the lawn mower again. "YOU GOT MY VOTE."

Natalie's long shadow led the way home. Her hopes of getting closer to Steven were dashed. So was her chance to run the School Store. Even though Steven wasn't asking for votes, he would get them because he was way more popular than Natalie. He would win the election, and so would Trina, and they would live happily ever after on Student Council, and in the yearbook photo, forever and ever.

That night after dinner, Annie phoned. She didn't say hello but simply launched into her two usual questions. *What did you have for dinner? Would you have traded it for hot dogs?*

"Beans with brown rice, and no," Natalie said.

"I would've traded the casserole Grandma Hatch made for hot dogs a million times over," whispered Annie. "We never have hot dogs. She says they're full of chemicals and ground-up pig noses."

Natalie sighed. "That's disgusting."

"What's wrong? You sound sad."

"I found out that Steven Redding is running for Student Council Secretary, just like me," Natalie said. "I was hoping he was running for treasurer, so we could both work at the School Store on Fridays. Now that's wrecked."

Annie chewed something crunchy — probably cheese puffs. "Olive, why are you running for Student Council? Is it because you want to sit next to a boy on Friday afternoons? Or because you love erasers and folders and pencils with every shaving of your being?"

"Both," Natalie confessed.

"Look. Steven will fall in love with you sooner or later. Who wouldn't? But for now, focus on your number-one dream: becoming Student Council Secretary. That *is* still your dream, right?"

Natalie took a deep breath, and imagined the spicy scent of freshly sharpened pencils. "Yes," she said. "But there's no chance of winning now. Steven will get all the votes."

"Not necessarily," Annie said. "To beat him, all you need is a great campaign."

"That's the other problem, Elvis. I'm supposed to make buttons and posters to promote myself. But first, I have to come up with a good campaign slogan, and I have no ideas."

"Don't freak out," Annie said. "I'll be your campaign manager."

"Really?"

"Sure. Step one: Let's come up with a great slogan. That will help you stand out."

Natalie was silent for a few seconds. "I can't think of anything," she moaned.

"Don't rush it. Good ideas come when they're ready."

"But you told Albert ideas were easy," Natalie said.

"Some ideas are trickier than others. Just like people." There was more crunching, then the sound of Annie licking her fingers. "Hey, good news. I discovered where my mom is."

"You did? How?"

"The coin, of course," Annie said. "It told me that she's living in Texas, Kentucky, and California."

"Hold on. How can someone live in three places at once?"

"Easy," Annie said. "She must have a job that forces her to travel around a lot. Is my mom an . . . FBI agent?" Natalie heard a slap. "Circus tent. No."

"She was a waitress before, right?" Natalie said. "Maybe she's a waitress now."

"Waitressing is a normal job, Olive. Nobody leaves

58

the person they're supposed to love the most to work at a normal job. She had to leave for a good reason," Annie said. "And maybe that reason is that she has a top-secret job she couldn't tell me about. Something that forces her to travel all over like an . . . astronaut?" *Slap.* "Nope."

Annie's mom, an astronaut? Was she *serious?*

"Now *you* think up some cool jobs she might have. Ask the coin about them, and I'll flip for you."

Natalie switched the phone receiver to her other ear. "Come on. This is silly."

"*Ask,*" Annie pleaded. There was a desperation in her voice that Natalie couldn't turn away from.

"All right," Natalie said. "Is Frances Beckett a . . . boat captain?"

There was a pause. "The coin says yes!" Annie cried. "Ask more."

"Is she a scuba diver?"

"Ooh, that's a good one." *Slap.* "Yes! What else?"

Natalie looked out her bedroom window. Over the rooftops, the setting sun had stained the sky the color of macaroni and cheese. "Is she a chef?"

59

"No."

"A writer?"

"Yes!" Annie said. "Wow. A boat captain who scuba dives and writes about it. That's a *great* job. I can see it now: She sets sail in Kentucky, floats to Texas, and then California, and back again. Along the way, she discovers new kinds of fish, and scientists admire her and beg her to come work for them. But no! She won't! Frances Beckett is too busy writing a book about her adventures."

Natalie sighed and sat down on her bed. First of all, it's impossible to sail from Kentucky to Texas. Second, Annie was bragging about her mom as if she was some kind of hero. But she had abandoned Annie, and had not been in contact for nearly two years. What kind of hero was that?

Annie was searching for a good reason why her mom left, but what if there wasn't one? Why couldn't Annie see that her mom returning was just one more hope, one more promise, that would surely be broken?

Chapter Six

The girls sat on Ms. Hatch's front stoop, a dwindling pile of tortilla chips on a napkin between them.

"I presented my Helping Hands project to Principal Tangleton today," Natalie said. "She said that finding lost flip-flops and writing song lyrics isn't helpful enough. If I don't come up with a better Helping Hands project in two days, I'm out of the running for secretary."

"Man, she's harsh," Annie said.

Natalie solemnly faced Annie. "Elvis, it's time to start collecting cans for the food shelf."

"*Or,*" Annie said, "we could simply solve bigger cases. Think how amazed your principal will be when she finds out you solved some real, live mysteries. That's much more impressive than soup cans."

Natalie stared up at the September sky, which was pencil-lead gray. "Fine. But we better find some big cases *soon*."

Annie took the last chip. "We will."

A strong wind stirred up a mini tornado of leaves and grit out in the street. Mr. and Mrs. Warsaw, the elderly couple who lived on Annie's side of the block, walked arm in arm down the sidewalk. Mrs. Warsaw's thin white hair blew across her face like wispy afternoon clouds. Mr. Warsaw tucked the flailing strands behind his wife's ear.

". . . and do you know what else, Charles?" Mrs. Warsaw said, coming into earshot. "She has hair down to her rear end, and it's as shiny as new pennies."

"Yes, my dove." Mr. Warsaw patted her hand. "Look, here's Natalie and Annie. Should we say hello?"

Mrs. Warsaw strolled over to where Natalie and Annie sat. "Hi! I'm Emily." She said it as if it was the first time she was introducing herself. As if she didn't say "Hi! I'm Emily" nearly every time they saw her.

"Hi," Natalie said. "We ate all the chips, but would you like some fruit leather?" She held out a strawberry-flavored leather.

"Yes!" said Mrs. Warsaw. "Thank you."

Mr. Warsaw gently took the treat from his wife. "I'll save it for later, all right?" He smiled sadly at Natalie. "She just took her medicine, and she has to wait at least an hour before eating."

Mrs. Warsaw mournfully watched the fruit leather disappear into her husband's pocket. "Zadie can eat whenever she wants. She doesn't take medicine."

"Who's Zadie?" Annie asked.

"Nobody," Mr. Warsaw whispered. "Someone Emily made up."

Mrs. Warsaw touched the hollow of her throat, then burst her arms open to the sky. "Zip! Zap! Zadie!"

A lot of what Mrs. Warsaw said and did lately made no sense. She took medication to slow the disease attacking her memory, but Natalie wasn't sure it was helping. One night at the end of the summer, Natalie and Annie had discovered Mrs. Warsaw wandering in her backyard, calling for a grandma who was surely long gone. Though they had led Mrs. Warsaw back inside her house that night, she seemed perpetually lost in the big backyard of her mind.

"My sweet cake, should we go home and take a nap?" Mr. Warsaw asked.

"All right." Mrs. Warsaw walked up the crumbly front steps of Annie's old house and headed for the porch.

"Darling, come back. That's not our house."

Mrs. Warsaw stopped and turned. "Of course it is. Right, girls?"

Natalie shook her head. "You live down the block, in the house with the blue shutters."

"Really?" Mrs. Warsaw looked extremely confused. "How do you know?"

"Because I see you and Mr. Warsaw come out the door for your afternoon walks."

"Plus, we're detectives," Annie said. "It's our job to know that kind of thing."

Mr. Warsaw folded his arms over his chest. "Detectives?" he said suspiciously. "That wouldn't have anything to do with spying, would it?" Mr. Warsaw hadn't been happy when he found out about the girls' spying club last summer.

"Nope," Annie said. "The E & O Detective Agency is a totally different club. We solve mysteries for the neighbors now."

"No more spying," Natalie reassured him. "Just helping. So if you need any help . . ."

Mr. Warsaw relaxed his arms. "I'll keep it in mind."

"Zadie," Mrs. Warsaw said to herself. "Zadie!"

"Come, darling." Mr. Warsaw put his arm around his wife and led her toward home.

Natalie caught a leaf as it fell from above. She studied the veins. "Getting old is no fun," she said.

"Yeah," said Annie. "What if that happens to Grandma Hatch?"

"Ms. Hatch isn't even seventy. Mrs. Warsaw is at least seventy-five."

Annie did some quick math on her fingertips. "So when she loses her mind, I'll only be fifteen."

"Not everyone gets dementia like Mrs. Warsaw."

"Even if Grandma Hatch does," Annie said, "I'll take care of her. Me and my mom will." Annie squinted at the sidewalk, suddenly lost in thought. Even though she was standing right next to Natalie, Annie seemed far away.

"Elvis, what are you thinking about?"

Ignoring the question, Annie pointed across the street. "Whose dog is that?"

A dog with fur nearly as orange and curly as a cheese puff was sniffing around the stop sign.

"I don't know," Natalie said. "I've never seen him before. Maybe he's lost."

A lost dog — now that was a big case. But would helping a lost dog home be good enough for tough Principal Tangleton? Would it count for extra that Natalie was allergic to dogs and helped anyway? Natalie wasn't sure, but she had to take a chance.

Time was running out to complete her Helping Hands project.

"Elvis," Natalie said, "the E & O Detective Agency is going to help that dog."

They approached the dog slowly, so they wouldn't spook him.

"Are you lost?" Natalie asked, letting the dog smell her hand.

Annie knelt on the grass, and the dog put a heavy paw on her thigh. "Oh, you wanna shake hands? Nice to meet you. What's your name?"

Annie reached for the tags on the dog's collar. He bounded backward and wagged his tail, begging her to try again. She lunged and missed. Natalie tried to grab the collar, too, but the dog was too fast and good at this game. They chased him in circles until they were breathless and needed to rest. The dog sat next to Annie on the sidewalk and leaned against her in a friendly way, his tongue dripping on her choir robe. Annie didn't seem to mind.

"You funny guy," she said, hugging him around the shoulders.

Drops began darkening the sidewalk, and they weren't from dog drool.

"Look, it's starting to rain," Natalie said. Lightning flashed, and there was a distant crack of thunder. "We can't leave this dog out here alone. But he can't stay at my house. Me and my dad are allergic."

Annie ran her small fingers through the forest of the dog's fur. "Want to come home with me? Huh?" He cocked his curly head at Annie.

"Will Ms. Hatch mind?"

"It's only for tonight," Annie said. "Meet me tomorrow after school in our headquarters, and we'll find out who he belongs to."

The rain was really coming down now. Annie hurried the dog onto Ms. Hatch's porch. Natalie pulled her jacket over her head and ran home.

The next day, Natalie sat in the club headquarters after school, waiting for Annie, who was late. While she waited, Natalie brainstormed campaign slogans on a clean sheet of notebook paper. So far, she had:

Vote for Natalie. She's sharp! (Drawing of a pencil)

Vote for Natalie. A cut above the rest! (Drawing of scissors)

They weren't bad slogans, but they weren't great. She drew a dark X over the entire page. Annie was better at coming up with ideas. Natalie should leave the brainstorming to her. Where was Annie, anyway?

The wooden board that served as a door to the headquarters rattled.

"Elvis?" Natalie said. "Is that you?" A wet, snuffling nose appeared through the hole. The dog wiggled his curly shoulders inside the headquarters and began galumphing around. Natalie sneezed twice.

"Grab his leash, Olive!" Annie's feet were visible just outside the headquarters. "He's hyper from eating candy."

The dog wore a pair of panty hose around his neck, the nylon feet dragging in the dirt behind him. Natalie grabbed the panty hose and, crawling on her hands and knees, led the dog out of the headquarters.

"I thought we were meeting at four to find the dog's owner. It's almost five," said Natalie, getting to her feet.

Annie took the homemade leash from Natalie. "I didn't mean to be late. But me and Grandma Hatch were having an argument. Our first fight."

"Why?" Natalie asked.

The dog lunged toward the sidewalk, knocking Annie off balance. Annie wrapped the panty hose leash around her wrist for a better grip.

"Last night, I wanted the dog to sleep in my bed, but Grandma Hatch said it wasn't allowed. Especially not muddy dogs. So I waited until she said good night, then I snuck him into my room."

"*Elvis,*" Natalie said.

"He was *lonely* out in the hallway," Annie insisted. "And hungry for cereal. You should've seen how happy he was under the covers, crunching Cheerios. Grandma Hatch discovered the muddy sheets while I was at school, and she wasn't happy when I got home. She said that if I live with her, I have to obey a few rules. I said a few is too many."

"Everyone has a *few* rules."

"Not my mom. She hates rules and so do I. That's why we should be together." Annie scrubbed the dog's back with her fingers. "You wanna live with us too, dog?"

"He already has a home," Natalie reminded her. "And we have to find it or I'm not going to pass my Helping Hands requirement. I told you: Principal Tangleton wants an update by tomorrow."

"Okay, okay," Annie said, letting the dog pull her down the sidewalk. The girls walked past Albert Castle, who sat on his front stoop eating a plate of apple slices.

"Do you recognize this dog?" they asked him.

"I'm sorry," he sang, *"but no."*

They stopped at the Gonzalezes' house.

"That's a golden doodle," Mrs. Gonzalez told them. "A cross between a golden retriever and a poodle. My sister has one."

"Did she lose it?" Natalie asked hopefully.

"No. And anyway, she lives in Mexico."

They asked more neighbors about the dog, but no one knew who he belonged to.

"Let him loose for a while," Natalie said. "Maybe he'll go home."

"Good idea." Annie dropped the panty hose. "Run, puppy. Run to your house."

The dog seemed to know the word "run," because he took off down the block. The feet of the panty hose danced wildly on the cement behind him.

TWEET! Noah Redding stepped from behind a tree and pointed an angry finger.

"No loose dogs!" he cried. "Ticket!"

"You can't give a dog a ticket," Natalie said.

"Watch me." Noah whipped out his little pink notepad.

Annie ignored all this. She was too busy laughing at the panty hose feet jumping behind the dog as he neared the intersection.

"Look both ways!" Natalie shouted as the dog charged across the street. Checking for cars, Natalie and Annie dashed after him, leaving Noah and his ticket behind. The dog ran for another block, then slowed. He stopped to sniff the lawn of a big blue house and trotted to the front door. He stared at the door handle with great expectation.

"Let's ring the bell," Annie said. "He's not going to do it."

The girl who answered the door looked about four years old.

"There you are!" she cried, hugging the dog around the neck. The girl wore red tap shoes and incredibly thick glasses that made her eyes appear large and swimmy. When she gazed up at Natalie and Annie, it was like she was looking through pool water.

"Where did you find him?" she asked.

"Two blocks away," Natalie said. "Make sure to keep him on a leash or inside so he doesn't get lost again, okay? What's your name?"

The girl blinked her large underwater eyes. "Millicent."

"Okay, Millicent?"

"Yes." The dog bounded out of her arms and into the living room, where he crash-landed on a sectional couch. "That's his favorite spot," Millicent said.

A teenage boy surfaced from the deep couch, a comic book dangling from one hand. He flipped his long, dark bangs out of his eyes. "Millie, who are you talking to?"

"Two girls. They found our dog."

"Oh, good," the boy said with little interest, then slumped back down into the couch cushions.

"That's my brother, Derek. He's babysitting me while my parents are at choir practice."

"What's your dog's name?" Natalie asked. "He wouldn't let us see his tags."

The girl tip-tapped onto the wooden threshold. She waved the girls in close for a whisper. *"Chicken."*

"Chicken?" Annie said loudly.

The dog's head shot up from his sunny spot on the couch. He jumped down and lumbered into the hallway, where he ran around Millicent in big dopey circles. Millicent tap-danced and waved her arms.

"You said his favorite word!" she crowed. "Now you owe him a treat."

Annie looked puzzled. "All I said was his name."

"He won't stop running till you give him some *chicken*," Millicent said. The magic word breathed new life into the dog's frenzy. He dashed down the hall and back, his toenails bunching the woven rug.

"All I have is some fruit leather," Natalie said. She quickly unwrapped the dried fruit strip and hurled it out the front door, where it bounced into the grass. Chicken crashed through the screen door and pounced on the treat. He lifted his head in thanks, the strawberry fruit leather hanging from his mouth like a second tongue.

"How did you know he was my dog?" asked Millicent.

"We have our methods," said Annie mysteriously. "We're detectives with the E & O Detective Agency."

The little girl looked them over with her amplified eyes. "Where are your badges?"

"Do you think we need some?" asked Annie.

"Yes." Millicent clapped for the dog. "Chi-Chi, come. We have to watch TV now."

"Can I give him a hug good-bye?" asked Annie.

"Sure."

Annie stroked the dog's curly ear-fur and rested her forehead against his. "It was nice to meet you, Chicken."

The dog squirmed out of Annie's arms. He ran into the hall and dashed around Millicent.

"Oops," Annie said. "I forgot."

"I don't have any more fruit leather!" Natalie said.

"Give him a chicken nugget from the freezer," Derek called irritably from the couch. "Mom keeps 'em in there just in case."

Millicent tap-danced into the kitchen. *"Chicken needs a nugget! Chicken needs a nugget!"* she sang.

Natalie and Annie showed themselves out. "Cross your fingers that this was enough for my Helping Hands project," Natalie said.

"I'm sure it will be." Annie took a good look at the clouds, which were puffed like popcorn that afternoon. "Millicent is right. We need badges."

Chapter Seven

Ms. Hatch was in the kitchen making soup when Annie and Natalie came in — it smelled like tomatoes and spice. Annie picked up an empty tomato can from the sink and twisted the tin lid free.

"Be careful, Annie," Ms. Hatch said. "That's sharp."

"I *know*." Annie did the same thing to a second can, and rinsed the two lids under the tap. "Do we have any cardboard?"

"In the recycling box in the hall closet." Ms. Hatch screwed the top off a spice jar and sniffed it. "Do you like rosemary?"

"What's rosemary?" Annie asked, digging through

the recycling. She found a thick piece of cardboard and tucked it under her arm.

"A spice," Natalie said. "It tastes good with tomato."

"It certainly does." Ms. Hatch stopped stirring the soup. "Did you find the dog's owner?"

"Yes," Annie said quietly. The afternoon's argument still hung in the air, as heavy as the smell of spice.

Ms. Hatch gave her a warm smile. "Thank you, firefly. And homework?"

Annie rolled her eyes. "I did it on the bus."

"Even the math worksheet you were having trouble with?"

"YES," said Annie.

"That's my girl." Ms. Hatch kissed the top of Annie's head. "Soup at six thirty."

Annie took the stairs two by two up to her bedroom and Natalie followed. Ms. Hatch didn't allow drawing on the walls as Ralph did, so Annie had taped her sketches to the purple-flowered wallpaper of her room. There were drawings of queens and kings, fields of flowers and horses, and castles with pointy towers. Annie was a great artist. A frilly violet canopy covered her bed, and under the canopy Annie had strung a dozen paper bats.

Natalie did what she always did when she came into Annie's room: She flopped down on the bed, stared up at the canopy, and said, "I wish this bed were mine."

"You can have it," Annie said. "It's way too girly for me. That's why I had to hang the bats."

"Did Ms. Hatch care?"

"No, she likes it when I do creative things. But she makes me go to bed by *ten*." Annie rummaged in a messy desk drawer.

"Lucky," said Natalie. "I'm in bed by nine."

Annie found a pair of scissors in the drawer and began snip-snipping through the cardboard. "She won't let me use the stove, which is dumb. I made macaroni and cheese for my mom almost every day." With each snip of the scissors, more cardboard shavings fell to the carpet.

"She just cares about you," Natalie said, sliding off the bed onto the carpet. "She doesn't want you to hurt yourself."

"I guess." Annie held up the two rectangles of cardboard she had cut out, each the size of a dollar bill. "These will be our detective badge wallets." She handed one to Natalie and kept one for herself.

Natalie picked up the two tin-can lids. "Are these going to be my campaign buttons?"

"No, those are our detective badges," Annie said. "We'll paint the wallets black, and once they're dry, we fold them in half. Then we glue the badge inside, like so. See?"

"That's a great idea!" Natalie said. "I hope you have ideas like this for my campaign. Have you thought of a good slogan yet?"

Annie tapped her head with the cardboard wallet. "It's still simmering up here, like soup."

"A few people are handing out buttons already," Natalie said. "If my Helping Hands project gets approved tomorrow, we should start making buttons immedia —"

"You worry too much," Annie interrupted. She gathered a bottle of glue, a permanent marker, a paintbrush, and a drippy pot of black paint from her desk drawer. "What I'm planning for you is *way* better than buttons. Leave it to me."

Natalie suggested they spread a piece of newspaper to protect the pretty purple carpet, then they got down to business. While Natalie painted her wallet with careful strokes, Annie painted with wild sweeps that spattered the newspaper. Out of nowhere, Annie started laughing.

"What's so funny?" Natalie asked.

"I was thinking about Chewlace, the dog me and my mom used to have. He was as obsessed about chewing shoelaces as Chicken is for chicken nuggets. Chewy made sure my laces were always cold and wet." Annie smiled. "Crazy dog."

Natalie fanned the air with her wallet, to help it dry faster. "Where is Chewy now?"

"After my mom left," Annie said, "the police found me and Chewy alone in the apartment. They brought us both to Ralph's house, but Ralph said no dogs. So the police took Chewy away in their squad car, and I never saw him again."

"That's sad."

"Not necessarily." Annie tested her wallet with a fingertip — the paint was nearly dry. "What if Chewy ran away from the police, and he chased after my mom and found her? Maybe he bit her shoelace so she couldn't escape again, and she laughed and said, 'Oh, Chewy' just like on a TV show."

"Come on, Elvis," Natalie said. "You don't really believe that's what happened."

"Why not?"

"Because this isn't a TV show. It's real life."

Annie leaned forward. "You want to know what really happened to Chewlace? The truth?"

"Yes," Natalie said. *Finally, the truth.*

Annie pulled the arcade coin from her pocket. "Let's find out."

Oh, no. More of this game?

"Did Chewlace chase after my mom?" Annie flipped the coin and clapped it onto the back of her hand. "Circus tent. That means no."

I could've told you that, Natalie thought.

"Hmm," Annie said. "Then what? Is Chewy still looking for my mom, like I am?" Flip. *Slap.* "Yes!"

"Elvis," Natalie said, "isn't there a better way to investigate your mom?"

"What do you mean?" Annie made a fist around the coin.

"Well, you said you want to figure out why your mom left and where she is. But you're asking an *arcade coin* questions. Maybe it's time to start asking yourself some questions."

Annie arched an eyebrow. "Like what?"

"Like, did your mom get into some kind of trouble that made her have to leave?"

"You don't know anything about my mom," Annie said, her voice as flat and cold as concrete.

"I know," Natalie said gently. "That's why I'm asking questions. Isn't that what good detectives do?"

"Right *now*," Annie said, "good detectives make badges." From the way Annie tossed a tin-can lid into Natalie's lap and turned toward her desk, Natalie understood: Annie was done talking about her mom.

Fine, Natalie thought. *Turn away from the truth. But it's still there.*

Annie uncapped the permanent marker, which stunk up the room. She studied the tin lid in her hand. "Our badges should say something official and impressive."

"How about 'Super Detective'?" Natalie said.

"Ooh, that's good." Annie squeaked the marker over the tin ridges. "Underneath I'm putting 'E & O Detective Agency.'"

Natalie copied the same things onto her tin lid. They folded the painted wallets in half, so they opened and closed like little books. Then they glued the badges inside and practiced using them. The trick was to get the wallet to flop open and reveal the badge inside at the perfect moment. It was all about timing.

"Good morning, ma'am," said Annie. "I'm Elvis of the E & O Detective Agency." *Flop.*

"No, it should be before you say your name," Natalie insisted. "That's more dramatic. Watch. Good afternoon, sir. I'm —" *Flop.* "Olive of the E & O Detective Agency."

"That's great!" Annie cheered. "We're real detectives now, just like Agent Milligan and Miss Dimesworth!"

The next day at school, Principal Tangleton, who had two Yorkshire terriers at home, was extremely touched that Natalie had helped a lost dog find its home. She approved Natalie's Helping Hands project on the spot. Her requirement fulfilled, Natalie didn't have to be a detective anymore. But why stop now? She liked helping people and dogs.

Over the next week, the E & O Detective Agency solved many cases. They found lost TV remotes in messy living rooms. They identified food that had been left too long in the fridge. They came up with new song titles for Albert Castle. Annie wore her tape mustache, which was slowly losing its stick. Natalie used her catchphrase whenever it seemed appropriate, but not so much that people would get sick of it.

The reputation of the E & O Detective Agency grew. Even neighbors Natalie had never talked to before started asking for help. One afternoon, a man called to them from a second-story window. "Are you Elvis and Olive? You have a detective agency?"

Flop. The girls flashed their badges in reply.

"I'm coming down," he said. In a few moments, Harold Reeves hurried out his front door in his stocking feet. He was a short, stubby man with a genuine mustache that Annie noticeably envied.

"Ms. Hatch told me you solve mysteries," Harold said.

"That we do." Annie's mustache dropped to the sidewalk, and she quickly pressed it back onto her face, crooked. "What's your mystery?"

Harold scratched his head, which was completely bald except for a half-wreath of hair that ended at each ear. "I lost a bag of books," he said. Harold was a librarian at the public library.

"Books?" Natalie's ears perked up like Chicken's. She loved books as much as school supplies.

"I only have a week to read those books," Harold said. "I have to find them today."

"Where did you see them last?" Annie asked.

In bright red socks, Harold padded toward his backyard. "I brought the bag home at lunchtime. I remember parking in the garage, then carrying the bag from the car, and then that bird . . ." Harold put his hands on his hips and looked around his yard mournfully. "Books, where are you?"

"What about the bird?" Natalie asked.

"Bird? Oh, there's a sparrow that sometimes flies circles around me when I come home. I think it's his way of reminding me to fill the bird feeder."

"What a smarty-pants," Annie said. "What happened next?"

"I checked the feeder to make sure it wasn't empty."

Annie pointed to the red bird feeder hanging from the fence. "You mean that feeder, with the grocery bag of books under it?" She grinned.

"Ha!" Harold cried, hurrying over to the brown paper bag. "I remember now. I set the bag down to add some more birdseed. Then the phone rang inside, and I ran to answer it. I forgot the books out here."

"Mystery solved!" Natalie said.

"You have good eyes," Harold told Annie.

"Thanks. I got them from my mom." Annie softly touched her eyelids.

Natalie peered into the grocery bag. "What are you reading?"

"Banned books." Harold pulled out a faded blue hardcover and brushed birdseed off the spine.

"Banned books?" Annie said. "What, outlawed books? *Criminal* books?" For the first time ever, Annie sounded interested in reading.

"Yeah," Harold said. "See, over the years, certain groups of people have tried to get rid of books they thought were no good. Thousands of books have been banned from libraries all over the world."

"Why do you have a bag full of criminal books?" Annie asked.

Harold laughed. "Today is the first day of National Banned Books Week. The other librarians and I are having a contest of who can read the most banned books before the week is over."

"But you're a librarian," said Natalie. "Why would you read a book that was banned from the library?"

"Because, like most librarians, I believe people deserve the freedom to read whatever they want."

Annie grabbed a thin green book from the bag. The cover said, *The Adventures of Tom Sawyer* by Mark Twain.

"That one has been removed from school libraries all over the country," Harold said.

"Why?" asked Natalie.

"Swearwords, among other things."

"Books can have swearwords?" A world of possibilities bloomed on Annie's face. She began flipping madly through the pages, no doubt searching for the dirty words.

"Were any books banned at our library?" asked Natalie.

"Yes. Back in the 1940s."

"Harold, can I borrow this?" Annie held up *Tom Sawyer.*

"Absolutely," he said. He gave Natalie a book to read, too: *Adventures of Huckleberry Finn*. "Just be sure to return them in two weeks, because they're checked out on my library card. Even librarians have to pay fines for late books." Harold picked up the bag and put it on his hip. "Stop by the library soon. I'll give you each a button for National Banned Books Week."

Natalie gave Annie a worried look. "Buttons, Elvis." Natalie was the only Student Council candidate who hadn't passed out buttons yet.

"Funny you should mention it," Annie said, developing a crafty smile. "I'm putting the finishing touches on your campaign stuff tonight. You are going to be so surprised."

Chapter Eight

It was mid October when a single leaf on the Wallises' maple tree shifted from green to orange. Almost overnight this one leaf, like a lit match, signaled the rest of the leaves on the maple to burn orange, red, and yellow. The color quickly spread to the other trees on the block, and within days of that first spark, all the leaves were blazing bright with the colors of fall.

Natalie leaned against the trunk of a particularly fiery maple at the bus stop and pretended to read the banned book Harold had lent her from the library. But really, she was watching Trina George carry an enormous flat white box toward the bus stop. Steven caught up with Trina and offered to carry one side of the box. Noah followed close behind, shouting warnings about twigs and pebbles in their path.

". . . because my cousin works there," said Trina, coming into Natalie's hearing range. "She's the head decorator — so she did it for half price."

"Nice," said Steven.

Trina flipped her hair over one shoulder. "But I had to give her one of my modeling headshots, which was so embarrassing." She giggled in a way that didn't sound very embarrassed.

Ricky Wallis dropped his backpack and ran up to Trina. "What's in that box?"

"I'll show you." Trina guided the box down to the grass, lifted the cardboard lid, and stood back so everyone could admire the contents. Natalie didn't want to care what was inside Trina's dumb box, and she wished she could stop herself from looking. But she did care. She looked.

The box held a huge white sheet cake with Trina's face drawn in frosting. Blond icing curled all over

Trina's head and tumbled gracefully down the sides of the cake. Her teeth were candy-coated pieces of gum and her lips a bright cherry gel. Pink cursive letters spelled, *Trina George for President. The answer to your prayers.*

"That's the biggest cake I've ever seen!" said Ricky.

"Pretty sweet," said Steven.

"I get it," said Noah, laughing. *"Sweet."*

Trina slid the lid back over the cake. "I'm handing out pieces during first and second lunch periods. Stop by."

At Trina's invitation, Steven's face turned the color of the frosting letters.

"Me too?" Ricky asked.

"Of course." Trina patted Ricky's head, then Noah's, and pointedly didn't invite Natalie to have some cake. Not that Natalie wanted to eat Trina's face, anyway. Punch it, more like.

Trina squinted at Natalie. "What are you staring at, snoop?"

"Nothing." Natalie's ears burned as she buried her gaze back in her book. Trina George had beautiful buttons, and now cake. She also had Steven's full devotion, even though she was too mean to deserve it.

Natalie stood beneath the flaming maple, shamed and cakeless, and waited for the bus to arrive. After what felt like forever, it rumbled up to the curb, and the door sighed open. Natalie waited behind Trina and Steven while they teeter-tottered the cake box up the steps of the bus. Natalie took her usual seat in the middle and rested her forehead against the cool windowpane.

As the bus chugged up the hill, it developed a strange clunking sound. At the next stop, Kelly, the driver, put the bus in park and opened the door.

"Sit tight while I check out that noise." She clomped down the steps. Billy Frohman climbed aboard the bus with his lumpy bag of hockey gear. Then, a second head bobbed up the steps. The hair was unevenly spiky and alarmingly familiar.

"Olive?" Annie Beckett stood in the aisle of Natalie's school bus, breathing hard as if she'd been running. She wiped a crown of sweat from her forehead into her hair. Annie was wearing her favorite pair of electric-blue overalls — the ones with the sticky gum stain on one knee. Natalie tried to say something, but her voice was suddenly gone.

"*There* you are," Annie said, and slid into the front seat with a brown-haired girl. "Olive, you have something on your tooth. Go like this." Annie rubbed her own front tooth.

"My name is Carol. And I have braces." The girl turned toward the window.

Annie jumped back into the aisle. "Oh! I saw the white shirt and blue skirt and . . ." She scanned the seats, filled with the uniformed students of Newton Academy. "Everyone is dressed alike. Which one of you is Olive?"

Natalie found her voice. "Over here."

Annie ran back to Natalie's seat, a paper grocery bag bumping each row she passed. She collapsed into the seat. "I forgot about the uniforms. I thought that girl was you! Wasn't that funny?"

Embarrassing, more like, Natalie thought. "What are you doing here, Elvis? You can't just jump on a bus that isn't yours."

"I wanted to surprise you." Annie patted the paper bag on her lap. "Your campaign stuff is ready."

"Really?" Natalie said. Kelly climbed back onto the bus and held up a long metal screw. "I've got a punctured front tire and a slow leak," she told the students as she restarted the engine. "But we'll make it to school."

"What's in that bag?" Natalie asked.

"Patience, girl. You'll see."

For one second, Natalie felt hopeful. Forget Trina's cake. Natalie had the world's most creative campaign manager on her side. Annie climbed onto her knees and faced the back of the bus.

"Hey, everybody," Annie said. "Listen up."

Natalie's hopeful second was over.

"Elvis, what are you doing? Sit down!" Natalie hissed.

Annie waved her away. "My best friend, Natalie Wallis, is running for Student Council Secretary. Every day, she surprises me with her brilliance, and I know she'd make the best secretary your school has ever had. Vote Natalie Wallis — she'll surprise you!"

On the word "surprise," Annie threw a handful of confetti toward the front of the bus. Then she turned to the back of the bus and did the same thing.

"Kid!" Kelly said. "Siddown."

Paying no attention to the driver, Annie sprinkled confetti over her own head, then Natalie's. The big boys in the last row burst out laughing. Natalie wished like crazy that she was invisible.

Kelly put on the brakes. She stomped down the aisle. "I said *siddown*." She put a heavy hand on Annie's shoulder, forcing her into the seat. "Do you go to Newton Academy?"

"Yeah, I'm going there now," said Annie.

"Are you *enrolled* there?"

"No."

"Then you can't be on this bus." Kelly snatched

the two-way radio from the sun visor above her seat. "Damion, I've got a boy on the bus who isn't one of mine. I didn't see him get on. What do you want me to do? Over."

The radio squawked. "Do you have time to take him back to where he got on?"

"I have a slow leak in my front tire," Kelly said. "I gotta go straight to the garage."

Squawk! "Once you get there, call his mom. She'll have to come pick him up."

"Okay." Kelly clipped the radio back onto the visor and shifted the bus out of park. Noah Redding raised his hand, and Kelly scowled at him in the rearview mirror. "What?"

"That's a girl, not a boy." Noah pointed at Annie. "And she lives with a foster mom, not a real mom."

"Foster grandma!" Annie shouted.

"You're lucky I don't have my tickets with me," Noah said. "Riding other people's buses isn't allowed."

"That's a *girl?*" said one of the boys in the back. "Now that's a surprise."

The bus erupted in laughter. Natalie was so humiliated and so mad — at Annie, at Noah, at the laughing kids. Hot tears were close. Oddly, the thing that stopped her from crying was seeing Annie's lower lip tremble.

"This wasn't how it was supposed to go," Annie whispered. She hugged the paper grocery bag on her lap.

Kelly adjusted the rearview mirror so she could see Annie better. "Hey, kid. Where do you really go to school?"

"Jefferson," Annie said.

"I'll drop you off there. It's on the way to the garage."

Annie slumped down in her seat, and so did Natalie. "What's in the bag?" Natalie asked gently. "Buttons?"

"Campaign favors. Way better than buttons."

"Did you make them?"

"Yeah," Annie said. "I wanted to hand them out at your school."

Kelly turned the final corner and pulled up to

Newton Academy. In a noisy bustle, everyone put on their backpacks.

"I can't hand out the favors anymore. *Unless . . .*" Annie said dangerously. Before Natalie could say wait, and before the other kids clogged the aisle, Annie shot to the front of the bus and flew out the open door, the grocery bag held high over her head.

"Hey! Get back on the bus!" yelled Kelly.

"Just a second," said Annie. As kids poured off the bus, Annie handed each a little brown bag from inside the big grocery bag and said, "Natalie for secretary. She'll surprise you. Vote Natalie. She's full of surprises."

One girl opened her bag and screamed.

"I bet you got the spider," Annie said. "Surprise!"

"Mine's a cookie shaped like a sword," said a boy. "Cool."

"I got some poop," said another boy.

"That's *clay*," said Annie. "You can make anything you want from it."

Natalie tried to push to the front of the bus to stop Annie. But there was a traffic jam of kids receiving their mortifying surprise bags. Trapped in the aisle, all Natalie could do was watch Annie through the window in horror. When one kid discovered a fistful of dirt in his bag, the possibility of being in charge of the School Store snapped like a cheap pencil.

Finally, the traffic jam loosened, and Natalie clomped down the bus steps. "What are you doing?" she demanded. "Trying to make me lose?"

"Of course not," said Annie. "I'm campaigning for you."

"By giving people spiders and dirt?" Natalie snatched the grocery bag away from Annie. "You're humiliating me!"

"It's not about the dirt itself," Annie said. "It's about the *surprise* of the dirt. Because you're surprising. Get it?"

"No, I don't. And I doubt anyone else does, either," Natalie said, gesturing to the circle of students that had formed around them.

Annie took a step closer to Natalie. "Trust me, Olive," she said softly. "I'm your campaign manager."

Natalie handed her the crumpled grocery bag. "Not anymore."

"You're *firing* me?" Annie shouted.

Suddenly, Kelly grabbed Annie's arm. "Okay, kid. Party's over."

"It sure is," Annie said as Kelly dragged her up the stairs of the bus. Annie's eyes were locked on Natalie's. "Meet me in the headquarters after school. We're not done talking about this."

Chapter Nine

After school, Annie and Natalie sat on opposite sides of the club headquarters. No one had bothered to light the candle. Unlike normal days, there was nothing to eat on the army blanket. This was no time for snacks.

"I stayed up *all night* making those surprise bags!" Annie yelled.

"Well, *all day* people kept pointing at me and saying 'There goes Dirt Girl.'"

Annie shook her head. "You fired the one person taking your campaign seriously. Good luck winning the election now!"

"What do you mean?" Natalie said. "I'm taking

my campaign *very* seriously. I've told you a million times that this is my dream."

"Ha. It's your dream, but you don't have the guts to make it come true. You're too scared to even come up with your own campaign slogan. What kind of a leader is that?"

"Oh, you want to talk about too scared?" Natalie said. "Let's talk about you, too chicken to ask yourself the questions about your mom that count. You're terrified of what you'll find out. So you ask a worthless game token ridiculous questions and believe the random answers. Your investigation is a joke."

Annie's eyes were ice-cold. "Just say what you've been thinking all along: You don't believe my mom is coming back."

It took all of Natalie's courage to match Annie's gaze. "No. Do you?"

"OF COURSE I DO!" Annie shouted. "If you knew anything about me by now, you would know that." Annie crawled toward the opening of the headquarters, the tops of her shoes dragging in the dirt.

Before she disappeared through the hole, Annie turned to glare at Natalie. "I'm going to find my mom, and when I do, you will feel so stupid."

At bedtime, the fight was still weighing Natalie down like a hundred bags of dirt. She brushed her teeth and got into her pajamas, and out of habit, grabbed her flashlight off the windowsill. *No,* she said, remembering the argument. *Not tonight.*

Since the end of the summer, Annie and Natalie had wished each other good night by shining flashlights into each other's windows. But after all the nasty things Annie had said about her, why should she say good night?

Natalie brought the flashlight to bed. She threw the covers over her head and shone the beam at the paint-chip lady on her headboard.

"I want to be Student Council Secretary more than anything," she whispered. "How dare Annie say I'm not taking myself seriously?"

As usual, the paint-chip lady didn't respond.

Natalie propped herself up on her elbows. "What, you think I'm not?"

Again, there was no answer.

Natalie didn't see Annie for two whole days. It was obvious that Annie was avoiding her. *Fine,* Natalie thought. *I'll avoid you, too.* On the third afternoon, Annie rang Natalie's doorbell. A late-afternoon shadow sliced across the screen, dividing Annie's face in two.

"Are you done ignoring me now?" Natalie asked. She played with the door latch, but didn't open it.

"I wasn't ignoring you," Annie said, not looking at Natalie. "I was grounded."

"Grounded? Why?"

"I took the city bus to Resselville the afternoon of our fight, to find some real answers." She crossed her arms. "You were right — my investigation *was* a joke. I decided to take the search more seriously."

"By taking the bus alone to Resselville?" Natalie said. "That's dangerous!"

Annie swatted away Natalie's concern like a fly. "I know that bus route by heart — me and my mom rode it all the time. I went straight to our old apartment to ask about my mom, but nobody knew anything. When it got late, I knocked on Henrietta's door — she's the apartment building's super — to ask if I could sleep on her couch and —"

"Ms. Hatch must have been dying with worry!" Natalie said.

"Henrietta made me call her to say I was okay. I told Grandma Hatch I'd bus home in the morning, but she insisted on picking me up right away."

"Elvis! Ms. Hatch had to drive to Resselville at *night*?" Natalie was too concerned to act angry anymore.

"Technically, it was morning by then — one A.M. Grandma Hatch was really mad. She grounded me for two days. No TV, no friends. But it was worth it, because I found this." Annie pressed a sky blue envelope to the screen door.

"What is that?" Natalie asked.

"A letter from my mom."

"For real? How did you get it?"

Even if she was still mad at Natalie, Annie couldn't help smiling now. "Henrietta said the letter came to my old apartment a couple months ago. She didn't know where I lived anymore, so she couldn't send it to me. But she kept the letter just in case I ever came back."

"Come in," Natalie said, finally unlatching the porch door. "Show it to me."

They sat at the white wicker table. With more care than Natalie had ever seen her use, Annie opened the envelope and pulled out the letter. She unfolded the light blue paper like it was the most fragile thing — a butterfly wing, maybe — and held it while Natalie read.

Baby? It's Mama.

I was a mess the last time I saw you, but I've cleaned up. I've changed. I'm getting some money together so I can come for you.

I'm not sure where you are now, so I'll send this letter to our old place and hope it will find you somehow. Write to me with

your address. We're going to have a brand-new life together, baby.
A fresh start. I promise.

I love you.

Mom

"See?" Annie said. "I told you she was coming back. This is proof."

Annie's shining eyes begged her to believe. And why shouldn't Natalie believe now? There it was — a real letter from Annie's mom with a real return address.

"You were right," Natalie admitted.

Annie smiled. "I knew she was looking for me, just like I was looking for her."

Annie's mom had made mistakes in the past, but people can change, right? Maybe Natalie had been wrong about Annie's mom. For Annie's sake, Natalie hoped so.

"Elvis, I'm sorry if I hurt your feelings the other day," Natalie said.

"Don't be. If you hadn't pushed me to look for the

truth, I would've never found this letter. I was afraid to go after the real answers." Annie picked at a loose piece of wicker on the armrest of her chair. "And I'm glad you fired me."

"You are?"

"Yep. It's better if you run the campaign yourself. That's what a real leader would do anyway," Annie said. "You *can* do this, Olive. I believe in you, and it's time you did, too."

A lump formed in Natalie's throat. Annie had faith in her, to the point of sacrificing her own feelings. Was she a good friend, or what?

Annie gently folded her mom's letter on the original creases. She slid the letter back in the envelope and tucked it beneath the waistband of her jeans.

"Does Ms. Hatch know about the letter?" Natalie asked.

"No," Annie said. "And I'm not telling her about the other letter, either."

"Which other letter?"

"The one you're going to help me write to my mom." Annie rocked in her wicker chair and grinned. "Right?"

Annie was counting on her. "Let me get some paper and an envelope from inside," Natalie said.

As the sun sank and left chilled shadows behind, Natalie helped Annie write a long letter to her mom. Annie described the neighborhood with its old houses and tall trees. She wrote about Ms. Hatch and how sweet she was. She wrote about her purple bedroom with the window that looked across the street to her best friend's house. Annie also told her mom about the E & O Detective Agency and the investigation that had led Annie to the letter.

Then Annie used a whole blank page to draw a house. "This is where we'll live," she said.

Natalie recognized the house numbers Annie had sketched on the door frame. "In Ralph's old place? Why there?"

"Good things happened to me when I was living in that house last summer," Annie said. "I met you.

I met Grandma Hatch. Even Ralph and Charla leaving — that was a good thing. It's a lucky house. A perfect place for a fresh start."

"But . . . it's falling apart," Natalie said.

"Me and my mom will fix it up," Annie said, and stuffed the fat letter into the envelope. On the front of the envelope, she copied her mom's address, pressing extra hard with the pen. Then Annie moved her hand to the upper left corner, to write the return address. Natalie stopped her.

"I think you should tell Ms. Hatch about the letters," Natalie said.

"No, not yet." Annie wrote her address bigger than necessary, then licked the envelope shut.

Chapter Ten

Annie believed that Natalie could win the Student Council election. So why couldn't Natalie start believing, too?

During second-period music, while half of the class learned to play the song "Rocky Top" on plastic recorders, Natalie drew a rectangle in her notebook. This was the School Store table. She drew the pencils and pens on one end and the folders on the opposite end, fanned out in rainbow order. The erasers went in the middle, organized according to smell.

Natalie happily sketched a stick figure with braids sitting behind the table. Even though her wish of running the School Store with Steven was impossible now, she drew a stick Steven sitting next to her stick self. Why not? This was her dream. The finishing touch was a line of customers so long, it spilled off the page. She *would* be elected secretary. She *would* run the School Store. She could feel it.

After music class, as Natalie passed the second-floor janitor's closet where the School Store supplies were kept, she dared herself to touch the doorknob. She imagined the weight of the closet key in her pocket. *Soon,* Natalie thought. *Soon.*

But during third-period history, Natalie's confidence was shaken by the loudspeaker.

"Attention students, this is Principal Tangleton. As part of this year's Student Council election, we're starting a new tradition. Each candidate will deliver a campaign speech during a schoolwide assembly at the end of October. All students will be excused from third period to attend."

Natalie's class erupted in cries of "All right, no history!" but Natalie didn't join the celebration. *Write a speech and deliver it to the whole school? Read it in front of Steven and Trina and Noah and all the teasing boys at the back of the bus — and all the teachers and even Principal Tangleton?* The thought was scarier than cafeteria meatballs. But Natalie would be brave like Annie and do it anyway.

At lunch, Natalie sat across the cafeteria table from Missy Reynolds, who had been her best friend last year. Missy primly opened her club sandwich like a book and leafed through the contents to remove the wilted pieces of lettuce.

Missy was dignified and proper — something Natalie used to hope for in a friend. But getting to know Annie over the summer had opened her mind. Natalie saw there were other wonderful things a friend could be — adventurous and funny and wildly different from herself. When school had started again, the polite friendship with Missy felt narrow and pinched, like Natalie's old cowboy boots. But Natalie kept being her friend anyway.

"Did you hear about Carol Fischer?" she asked Natalie. "She bit into a cookie that your friend gave out on the bus. It was so hard, she broke a braces wire."

Natalie cringed. "That's awful."

"Your campaign manager is making you look bad." Missy tweezed a limp lettuce leaf from her sandwich. "She's wrecking your chances of getting elected."

"Annie isn't my manager anymore," Natalie said. "I am."

"You're going to be your *own* manager? Nobody does that." Missy wiped her fingers on her napkin. "Do you really think you can write your own speech?"

"It's scary," Natalie agreed, reaching into her lunch bag for a banana. "But I can do it."

Missy rested her forearms on the table. "I'll be very honest with you. It's impossible to write a speech unless you have experience. My dad will tell you himself: He only got elected to City Council because he took a speech-writing workshop. The first time he ran, he wrote his own speeches and *lost*."

"But I'm a good writer already," Natalie said. "I get As on all my book reports."

"Writing isn't even the hardest part," Missy said. "Standing in front of hundreds of people is.

Imagine — there are twice as many eyeballs as people, all staring at you. If a speech coach doesn't prepare you for that moment, you could freeze up. Or worse: faint."

Natalie bit her lip. "It's only for a minute. It'll be over before I know it."

"Exactly," Missy said. "You only have one minute to convince everybody to vote for you. If you waste that minute saying the wrong thing, or fainting, you could destroy your chances of being elected secretary."

"I didn't think of it that way," Natalie said, now too terrified to even peel her banana.

"It's simple: I'll be your new campaign manager and help you write your speech. I know all kinds of techniques from watching my dad. I'll make great campaign buttons and posters. And I won't embarrass you like that dumb neighbor girl did."

"Annie's not dumb," Natalie said. "She's my best friend, and she was only trying to help."

Missy shrugged and took a bite of her neatly edited sandwich. "If you want to win, trying isn't good enough. You *do* still want to become Student Council Secretary and run the School Store, don't you?"

School Store. The words twanged the guitar strings of Natalie's heart, playing a chord full of longing. What if Missy was right about the speech, and preparing it herself would doom Natalie to failure? Could she risk refusing Missy's help?

Missy clasped her hands tidily under her chin. "So, are we partners?"

Natalie smiled weakly. "Yes."

When the bus pulled up to Natalie's block, Annie was standing on the corner, waiting for Natalie with her badge wallet in one hand. Kelly the driver opened the door to let kids off and jumped when she saw Annie standing on the curb in her choir robe and phony mustache.

"Not you again!" Kelly shrieked. "Stay off my bus."

"I told you," Annie said. "I spilled your coffee thermos on *accident*. Once again, I apologize."

"Ha!" Kelly waited for the kids to get off the bus, then sped away.

Annie shrugged, then turned to Natalie. "Sergeant Dewey has a case for us to solve. Go get your badge."

Nathaniel Dewey was an army sergeant who lived alone in the green-and-white house two doors down from Natalie. He fought in a war a long time ago, and now he trained the younger soldiers. When he wasn't out of town on training missions, Sergeant Dewey was often in his backyard, lifting weights. Or, as the girls discovered last summer, he sometimes made papier-mâché hot air balloons in his basement.

Natalie ran up to her bedroom and grabbed the badge off her desk. When she came back outside, Annie was already on Sergeant Dewey's front stoop.

"Come on, leader," Annie said. "You knock this time."

The word "leader" made Natalie's stomach flip-flop. Annie didn't know that Missy was her new campaign manager. Would Annie be mad when she found out? Natalie had to find a way to tell her that wouldn't hurt her feelings. She would . . . later. For now, Natalie rapped the brass bulldog knocker on Sergeant Dewey's door.

Sergeant Dewey yanked open the door as if he'd been waiting all day. He chewed a carrot stick as if it had somehow offended him.

"So you're detectives now, huh?" he said. The girls flashed their tin-can badges.

"Tell me: Who stapled this to my maple tree?" He handed Natalie a piece of paper. It read:

NEW LAWS
1. *Crossing the street wile eating = 1 ticket*
2. *Girls out after dark = 1 ticket*
3. *Wearing strong profume = 2 tickets*
4. *3 tickets = a ride in the squade car + jail*
Sincelery,
The Sheriff

Natalie giggled. "I guess there's no law against bad spelling. 'Sincelery,'" she said. "Celery!"

Annie grabbed the note. She smelled it, as if that was an important part of her investigation. "Just as I thought," she said.

"Smells like celery?" asked Sergeant Dewey.

"No," said Annie, "it smells like trouble. Sergeant Dewey, this note is from Noah Redding, who has made himself the sheriff of our block. But he's not a real sheriff, so these aren't real laws."

"Well, he *really* stapled them to all the trees on our street," said Sergeant Dewey. Flyers fluttered on maple trees up and down the block.

"That no-good maple stapler," Annie said. "Excuse us, Sergeant Dewey. We're going to pay the sheriff a little visit."

Noah was standing watch in his front yard while Steven raked leaves.

"I want a pile of red and a pile of yellow," Noah commanded. "Stop mixing them!"

Steven pointed his rake at Noah like a giant claw. "Say that again."

Noah held up his hands in surrender. But when

Steven turned away, Noah mumbled, "No rake point-ing. That's number one on next week's laws."

"Get a life, man," Steven said, and circled around to the backyard.

"Noah!" Natalie shouted, waving the flyer. "We need to talk to you."

"Sheriff," Noah said with maddening calm. "My name is Sheriff."

"Whatever," Annie said. "You can't staple your flyers to trees."

Noah kicked Steven's pile of leaves. "I make the rules around here. If I want to staple some things to other things, I can."

"Are you going to take down the signs or not?" asked Annie.

"Not."

"Then we will." Annie said. She tore the flyer from the nearest tree and clapped it into a wad.

Noah sauntered over to her. "There's going to be a law against girls with short, homemade haircuts and fake mustaches."

"Careful," Annie said menacingly and took a step toward Noah. "Or I'm going to tell everyone your big secret."

Noah's eyes narrowed and shifted between the girls. At the end of the summer, Annie got Noah off their case by saying she knew a big secret about him, and if he didn't cool it, she'd spread it around. In truth, Annie didn't have any dirt on Noah, but the fact that he acted so scared made it clear that there *was* a secret. Annie had no idea what it was and neither did Natalie, but Noah didn't need to know that.

"You're the one who should be careful," Noah said. He poked her in the belly and there was a crinkly noise. Natalie knew that Annie kept her mom's letter hidden under her waistband. It was a part of her daily wardrobe now, like underwear and socks.

"Careful is one thing I'm not," Annie said. She and Noah stood nose to nose, neither one moving. The only sound was of two squirrels chasing each other up the big oak tree on the boulevard.

"Zadie!" Mrs. Warsaw screeched from across the street. "Zadie would stop that fight so fast, nobody would have a chance to land a punch!"

"What's wrong?" said Mr. Warsaw, rushing out his front door. "Why all the shouting, sweet pea?"

"There was almost a fight," said Mrs. Warsaw. She pointed at Annie. "That girl was about to cream that little boy."

Noah scowled and crossed his arms. "It's the other way around."

"Annie and Noah were just arguing. Nobody's going to fight today." Natalie turned to Noah. "Right, Mr. Secret?"

Noah backed away from the girls with a sinister *fip-fip* of his pants. "I'll get you later," he said with a mean smile and ran into his backyard.

Natalie and Annie crossed the street to where Mrs. Warsaw was standing on the sidewalk, her eyes wide. "Zadie is good at stopping fights. She's tall and strong and she only wears purple," Mrs. Warsaw said and punched the air with a bony fist. "Zip! Zap! Zadie!"

Mr. Warsaw, who stood a few paces back on the leaf-littered lawn, sighed. "My love," he said gently. "Let's go inside."

"Good idea!" said Mrs. Warsaw. "I'll introduce these girls to Zadie. I'm Emily. What are your names?"

"You can call me Elvis," said Annie.

"I'm Olive."

Mrs. Warsaw took them each by the hand. "Elvis and Olive, it's time to meet Zadie."

Chapter Eleven

M r. Warsaw tried to convince his wife to have some tea in the kitchen. Or rest in her favorite chair in the sunroom. But she wouldn't hear of it. She tugged Natalie and Annie toward the carpeted stairs to the second floor.

Mr. Warsaw started to follow them, but his wife shooed him away. "You're not invited, mister! This is lady business."

"Okay, sugar," he said. "Girls, take care that she doesn't fall on the stairs."

Natalie offered her shoulder to Mrs. Warsaw for support. At the top of the steps, the old woman reached for the crystal doorknob of a closed bedroom door. "It's time I share the secret," she whispered. "I've been hiding Zadie in my closet."

"But who *is* Zadie?" Natalie asked.

"You'll see." Inside the room were two twin beds with peach-colored bedspreads. Mrs. Warsaw sat on one of the beds. "You have to promise not to tell my mother anything. She'll be mad if she finds out."

Mrs. Warsaw was old. Her mom was probably dead by now. Their promise to not tell her anything would be easy to keep.

"Shut the bedroom door," Mrs. Warsaw said. "And open the closet. That's where Zadie is."

Annie turned the doorknob and eased open the closet door. Natalie held her breath and waited for a giant lady dressed in purple to jump out. Annie ruffled through the row of blouses and slacks hanging there, which smelled of ancient soap.

"I don't see anyone," Annie said. "Do you, Emily?"

"Of course not. You think I'm crazy?" Mrs. Warsaw said. "Look *behind* the clothes."

Natalie pushed aside the hanging clothes while

Annie checked the back of the closet. "Nobody's here," said Annie.

"I'll show you," Mrs. Warsaw said, slowly standing up from the bed. Steadying herself against Natalie, the woman reached deep into the closet. She tapped the back wall. Then her hopeful expression melted into sadness.

"Zadie was in here," she said, starting to cry. "I'm sure of it." She wiped her runny nose on her sleeve.

The bedroom door opened with a soft click. Mr. Warsaw, who had apparently been listening the whole time, stepped into the room. He sat Emily on the bed and put his arm around her.

"It's all right, dove," he said.

"We didn't mean to make her cry," Natalie said.

"It's not your fault. We go through this almost every day." Mr. Warsaw rubbed soft circles on his wife's back. "Emily is convinced there's a woman hiding in our closet, but it's all in her mind."

Mrs. Warsaw rested her head against her husband's neck. "It's not just any woman. It's Zadie."

"She brought Virginia Brooks up here to show her, and that little Turner girl from across the street. But the same thing happens each time. When she sees there's no one in the closet, she gets upset."

"What can we do to help?" asked Natalie.

Mr. Warsaw stroked his wife's hair. "Nothing, really," he said. "The doctor wants to try a new medication to see if it will make a difference. But it costs much more than what we're paying now."

"Maybe my dad can give you a discount," said Natalie. Mr. Wallis was a pharmacist at the Rexall Drug Store.

"That's thoughtful," he said. "But I'm afraid health insurance doesn't work that way."

Mrs. Warsaw sniffled, and her husband patted her hand and said, "I'm going to fetch you a tissue, love bug."

When he left the room in search of a tissue, Mrs. Warsaw's gaze suddenly cleared, like the sun peeking through constant clouds.

"Something is wrong with my mind," she told the girls. "Have you noticed?"

"Yes," Natalie admitted.

"It makes me afraid. If I could see Zadie, she could help me. She helps everybody." Her eyes flooded with tears again, and she reached for Natalie's hand. "I *must* see her."

"What did you have for dinner? Would you have traded it for hot dogs?"

"Whole wheat spaghetti, and no," Natalie said, shifting the telephone to her right ear. "Maybe. I don't know. I wasn't hungry because I couldn't stop thinking about Emily. I wish there was a way to help her."

"There is," said Annie. "Finding that Zadie lady."

"Zadie is someone Emily made up," Natalie said. "Mr. Warsaw said so."

"Maybe, maybe not," said Annie. "Emily is convinced she's real."

"But her mind is all foggy. She told us herself," said Natalie.

"She also said that Zadie could help her somehow. What if she's right? Shouldn't we try to lend a helping hand, Miss Secretary?"

"You're right." Natalie rubbed the lacy edge of her bedroom curtains, the ones her mom had sewn last July. "I guess Zadie could be a doctor. Or a therapist. Or a friend. Although I don't understand the part about hiding in Emily's closet."

"It's a mystery all right, and it's our duty to investigate," Annie said. "As Miss Dimesworth says, the answer to every mystery is out there, as long as you ask the right questions."

The next day was Saturday, so Natalie and Annie had all day to investigate Zadie. They started right after breakfast, at Sergeant Dewey's door.

"Yes?" The sergeant answered his door holding a basket of freshly laundered socks.

Annie and Natalie flopped their badges open. "Can we ask you a few questions?"

"Shoot."

"Have you ever heard of someone named Zadie?" Natalie asked. "She supposedly is very tall, has hair down to her behind, and is good at stopping fights."

"No. Sounds like my kind of woman, though."

Natalie made a note of it.

"Thanks anyways," said Annie, and turned to leave.

"Is that all?" Sergeant Dewey gave them a severe look. "You said a *few* questions. That was only two."

Annie stroked her taped-on mustache. "Okay. If you had to eat the same thing for breakfast every day for the rest of your life, would you choose (a) cereal, (b) doughnuts, or (c) hot dogs?"

Sergeant Dewey cracked a rare smile. "Cereal. The kind with crunchy marshmallows."

The girls knocked on Ms. Brooks's door next. As usual, she only opened it a crack.

"I don't want to buy any cookies or wrapping paper. . . . Oh, it's you girls." Ms. Brooks swung the door open. She wore the same faded silk kimono as always.

Natalie and Annie flashed their badges. "We're here to ask some questions, like you taught us to do," Natalie said.

Ms. Brooks nodded proudly. "Ask away."

"Have you ever heard of a lady named Zadie?" Annie asked.

"Zadie? Oh my, yes. Emily goes on about her when we have tea on Thursdays. She says . . ." Ms. Brooks hesitated.

"What?"

"She says this Zadie person wears a crystal necklace that magnifies her 'natural powers.' Apparently, the crystal changes colors when she 'flies.'" Ms. Brooks gave a small snort of disbelief.

"She *flies*? That's a great clue!" Annie said as Natalie jotted it down. "We're going to crack this case soon — I can feel it. Can you feel it, Miss Dimesworth?"

Ms. Brooks's painted-on eyebrows slanted with sadness. Her chin wobbled.

"Is anything the matter?" Natalie asked.

"It's just . . . I used to be adventurous like you girls. I used to be *somebody*," Ms. Brooks said tearfully. "Now I'm nobody."

Annie gaped at her. "Are you joking? You're *Miss Dimesworth*."

Ms. Brooks shook her head. "Not anymore."

"You are to me," Annie said fiercely. Ms. Brooks scurried back inside her house, insisting she had things to do.

Natalie and Annie rang doorbells all afternoon, flashing their badges and asking everybody what they knew about Zadie. Every so often, Annie threw in the breakfast quiz for fun. A lot of people had heard of Zadie, but only because Mrs. Warsaw had told them things. She told Albert that Zadie could run faster than a cheetah, and Albert had composed a jingle about it:

Zadie runs like cheetahs
On zipping, zapping feet-ahs.

Mrs. Warsaw had told Sandy and Leena, the women who lived on the corner, that Zadie slept in a stream at the foot of a volcano.

After they had interviewed everyone on their own street, Natalie and Annie walked two blocks down. In front of Millicent's house, Chicken the dog was lying on the front lawn, belly up, looking enormously pleased with himself and a little sick.

Natalie rang the doorbell, and Millicent answered.

"The detectives," Millicent said, blinking her wide eyes.

"We're here on official business," Natalie said, and flopped open her badge.

"Have you ever heard of a person named Zadie?" Annie asked.

"No," Millicent said. "Have you ever heard of a dog who can steal a loaf of bread from the countertop and eat the whole thing?" She pointed an accusing finger at Chicken.

Annie knelt by the dog. She rubbed his belly and

spoke to him softly. "We're looking for Zadie. Have you seen her, Chi-Chi?"

"Dogs are good at finding people on TV," said Millicent. "Give him something of Zadie's to sniff and maybe he'll find her."

"That's the problem," Natalie said. "We don't have anything of hers. All we have are some notes."

Millicent sat on the front steps. "Read Chi-Chi the notes, then."

Natalie didn't think that reading the dog her detective notes would make any difference, but Millicent was looking up at her with those adorable underwater eyes. Plus, Annie wasn't done petting the dog. Natalie flipped open her notebook.

"Zadie can run faster than a cheetah. She sleeps near a volcano. She wears a crystal necklace that makes her powers stronger. Oh, and she flies." As Natalie read, Chicken shamelessly ignored her. "What does this tell us about Zadie?"

Annie sat up on her knees. "That Zadie is amazing."

"That she isn't a real person, Elvis. No real person can outrun a cheetah or fly." Natalie put the notebook in her jacket pocket. "Zadie doesn't exist. She's a part of Mrs. Warsaw's imagination, and that's it."

"Wait. Maybe Zadie isn't a real person, but she still can exist."

"How?"

Annie jumped to her feet. "Does Superman exist? Does Spider-Man exist?"

"Yes," said Natalie, "but only as fictional superheroes."

"*Exactly.* What if Zadie is a superhero?"

"Like in a comic book?" Millicent asked.

"Yes!" Annie cried.

"Hmm," said Natalie, resting her pencil eraser thoughtfully against her lips.

Millicent ran to the front door. "DEREK! Come here."

In a minute, Millicent's teenage brother Derek padded down the stairs in socks that flopped with every step. "I'm in the middle of a game," he grumbled, his eyes hidden under long bangs. "What?"

"These girls are looking for a lady who might be a superhero," said Millicent.

"Do you know a lot about superheroes?" Natalie ventured.

With a jerk of his head, Derek flipped his bangs out of his eyes and glared. "Uh, *yeah*. I volunteer at Comic-Con. Biggest comic book convention in the country."

Annie stepped into the doorway. "Is there a comic book character named Zadie?"

Derek's scowl morphed into curiosity. "I'm not sure. Let's check."

The first thing Natalie noticed about Derek Takeda's room was the smell, like a blast of hot Doritos breath. The second thing was the wall of comic books. Some of the spines were printed in Japanese and the rest in English. Each comic wore a little plastic jacket.

"Awesome," said Annie, running a fingertip along the plastic-covered spines.

"Do *not* touch those," said Derek. "A comic's value comes from its condition. Mine are *mint,* and I'd like to keep them that way."

Using both hands, Derek pulled a heavy book off the shelf. *Encyclopedia of Superheroes* announced the cover in big red letters. He sat on his unmade bed and opened the book to the last few pages.

"Zabertron, Zachery Zoom . . . here we go: Zadie Zeolite."

Natalie and Annie peered over Derek's shoulder as he read the encyclopedia entry out loud:

"'Zadie Zeolite was discovered in a crystal-filled stream at the bottom of a volcano bordering the Caribbean Sea. Raised by a local family as a normal child, it quickly became clear that she had special powers.

"'When she was ten, Zadie taught herself to run faster than a cheetah. At age twelve, she learned to fly. At fifteen, she discovered her greatest power: crystallization. Zadie Zeolite can crystallize a punch being thrown, making the fist motionless and powerless, or immobilize the legs of a fleeing criminal. To perform a crystallization, Zadie touches her crystal necklace and shouts, "Zip! Zap! Zadie!"'"

"That's what Mrs. Warsaw always says!" Annie cried.

Derek glared at her. "Do you want me to finish reading or not?"

"Please."

"Then listen," said Derek. "'Zadie Zeolite is credited as being the very first female superhero. She starred in nine comics in 1940, the year of her creator Harriet Jones's death. The only known surviving copy of *The Adventures of Zadie Zeolite* is held at Marvin Studios in New York City.'"

As Derek read, Natalie took speedy notes. Annie rested her forearm on Derek's shoulder, before he shrugged it off.

"How come there's no picture of Zadie?" Annie asked. "There are pictures of the other superheroes."

"To include a picture in this encyclopedia, Marvin Studios would need to lend their copy of *Zadie* to the publisher. If you only had one copy of something, would you lend it out?"

"No," Natalie said. "It might get damaged. Or lost."

"Precisely."

"If Zadie is such a big deal," said Annie, "how come no one's ever heard of her?"

Derek flipped to the index at the back of the book and ran a finger down the Z column. There was nothing else on Zadie in the whole encyclopedia. "I'm not sure why," he said. "Maybe because the creator died soon after the comic started. Or maybe kids didn't like her necklace. How the heck should I know?"

"All the other comic book series have prices underneath them, but Zadie's doesn't," Natalie pointed out.

"That's because there aren't any copies for sale," said Derek. "If there *were*, they'd be worth a lot of money."

"But you just said it wasn't a popular comic."

"Exactly, so the copies are rare. In the collecting world, rare means valuable." Derek slid the hefty encyclopedia back onto the shelf. "Plus, if Zadie really was the first female superhero, that would mean something to collectors."

"How much money are we talking?" asked Annie.

"Let me put it this way," Derek said, shaking a can of lime soda. "A rare Spider-Man comic in mint condition was auctioned for more than two hundred thousand dollars. Zadie's not as hot as Spider-Man, but she's older and way more rare." He opened the soda and took a swig of the fizz. "I can't say for sure, but if you put a ray gun to my head, I'd guess a Zadie comic would sell for a hundred grand."

"A hundred thousand dollars for a *comic book?*" Natalie asked.

Derek flipped his bangs out of his eyes. "A hundred grand *at least*."

Outside, the dried leaves made a crunchy carpet on the sidewalk, and every step gave off a sweet, toasty smell. As Natalie and Annie walked home, they discussed the case.

"No one believed Emily," Annie said, "but now we know she was telling the truth. Zadie exists."

"And we can guess that she was looking for Zadie comic books in her closet."

"Yes." Annie shuffled her feet through the leaves. "But there aren't any. We saw that ourselves."

"Yeah. The only things in her closet are clothes and shoes." Natalie put her hands in her pockets.

"It's too bad. Zadie comics would be worth a lot of money."

"Emily doesn't want money," Natalie said. "She just wants to see Zadie again. It's a shame there wasn't a picture of Zadie in Derek's encyclopedia."

"We'll keep searching."

Chapter Twelve

At school on Monday, Missy surprised Natalie with a big, white envelope.

"Open it," Missy said, barely able to contain her excitement.

"Are these buttons?" Natalie felt inside the envelope. The button she pulled out was a square of plain white paper, printed with black block letters that said, *VOTE NATALIE FOR SECRETARY.*

"I made them square because it wastes less paper than round," Missy bounced on her heels. "Aren't they nice?"

"They're great," Natalie said. Her upper lip twitched, as it always did when she told a lie.

Natalie hadn't made the buttons, so who was she to complain that they were a little boring? If Natalie *had* made them, she might have cut them round anyway and added some color. But Missy was the campaign manager, so she got to decide.

"Let's hang your poster before first bell," Missy said, drawing a long white tube from her backpack. They hurried to the wall outside the principal's office, where all the campaign posters hung. Clara Winkle's sign featured her name in rainbow bubble letters, a drawing of a lightbulb, and the phrase *Clara for Secretary. She's bright!* A boy running for vice president had a poster announcing *We Agree, Vince for VP,* with colorful cartoon faces surrounding the blue words. Trina's poster wasn't made with markers, of course. It was professionally printed with a large photo of Trina's face, looking as proud and flawless as ever. The pink type said, *Vote Trina for President. The answer to your prayers!*

For the poster Missy made, Natalie didn't expect anything close to Trina's glossy sign. But she didn't expect what Missy was now taping to the wall, either.

It was the button, only bigger. Square and plain white, with towering black letters spelling out *VOTE NATALIE FOR SECRETARY*. It certainly wasn't embarrassing like Annie's surprise bags, but the poster was, well, *dull*. There was no slogan. No color. No personality. If the poster and buttons could speak out loud, they would sound like robots.

"Do you like it?" Missy asked cautiously.

"Of course," Natalie said, her lip twitching. "Thank you!"

"Your mom's pumpkin bread is *so* delicious," Annie said. She and Natalie sat in the Wallises' dining room, having an after-school snack of fresh pumpkin bread and soymilk. "You could pass out slices as campaign favors. But only if you want to. You're the campaign manager — it's up to you."

Natalie's lip twitched hard. She still hadn't found a way to tell Annie that, actually, she wasn't her own manager. And according to her twitching lip, avoiding the truth was the same as lying.

Annie nodded at Natalie's shirt. "I see you made campaign buttons. They're very . . . to the point."

Natalie took a deep breath. "Elvis, I have to tell you something. Remember how I said I was going to be my own campaign manager?"

"Yeah. Remember how I said I was glad you were taking charge?"

"Missy Reynolds scared me into making her my new campaign manager," Natalie blurted. "I'm sorry I didn't tell you right away. I was afraid you'd be mad." Natalie braced herself for Annie to do something crazy, like throw her glass of soymilk in Natalie's face.

But all Annie did was calmly take a bite of pumpkin bread. "It's your campaign," she said. "You can hire and fire whoever you want. That's not the problem."

"It's not?"

"The problem is being afraid all the time. You worry too much about what everyone thinks." Annie tapped Natalie hard on the breastbone. "Trust yourself, Olive."

"I want to," Natalie said solemnly.

"Then do it." Annie began carving superhero swoops in the air with her crust of pumpkin bread. "And now, back to our regularly scheduled program: The Case of Zadie Zeolite!"

"Have you discovered anything new?"

"No," Annie said, still flying around the dining room table. "We need to hunt for more clues."

"But where? From who? We interviewed all of our neighbors already."

"Don't worry. Something will occur to us soon." Annie grinned expectantly at Natalie. "*Occur.* You like that word? I learned it in my banned book."

"Don't tell me you haven't returned *Tom Sawyer* to the library yet," Natalie said. "I think it's overdue. Harold will get a fine."

"But it's the first book I've ever liked," Annie said. "I've decided to keep it."

Natalie laughed. "Library books are just for borrowing. But I'll buy you your own copy for your birthday."

"Oh, all right," said Annie. "Let's return it now."

"Hi, Harold," Natalie whispered across the librarian's desk.

"Ah, the detectives," said Harold. He was checking in a messy stack of children's picture books.

Annie slid *Tom Sawyer* on top of the stack. "Sorry if this is late."

Harold scanned the book with a beep. "It's due today, so there's no fine. Here, have a button." He handed them each a button that said, *I Heart Banned Books!*

"Thanks, Harold," Natalie said, pinning hers next to Missy's paper button.

"I know National Banned Books Week is over," Annie said, a little too loudly for a library, "but do you have any more banned stuff I could read?"

Natalie couldn't help grinning. *Elvis hearts books!*

"Of course. I haven't reshelved these yet." Harold wheeled a metal cart from behind the desk. The girls began thumbing through the titles.

"You told us that some books were banned at this library back in the 1940s," Natalie said. "Were they these books?"

"Actually, no," Harold said. "Funny enough, at our library, the only materials ever banned were comic books."

"Comic books?" Annie nearly shouted. She stroked her mustache pensively, and Natalie guessed they were both wondering the same thing: What if *The Adventures of Zadie Zeolite* was one of the banned comics?

"Harold," Natalie said, "tell us more."

He sat on his stool. "Let's see. In 1945, a group of parents in our city decided that comic books were dangerous. They thought all those superhero kicks and punches would make their children violent. So they started a petition to have the comics removed from the library, and a lot of people signed it. The head librarian did what the public demanded. She got rid of every single comic book."

"Got rid of them how?" Natalie asked.

Harold sucked his teeth. "That's hard to say. They

might've been burned, but I doubt it. I bet they were thrown in the trash."

"In the Dumpster out back?" Annie asked.

"Most likely."

Annie zipped up her jacket. "Olive, let's go check."

"The comics were disposed of decades ago," Harold said apologetically. "There's a trash pickup every week, so . . ."

"So even if they were thrown in the Dumpster," Natalie said, "they're long gone."

"Correct," said Harold.

Annie crossed her arms. "Darn. Time for more questions."

"Questions," Natalie echoed. "Let's see: Who started the petition to have the comics banned?"

"The Doty Morality Society," Harold said. "According to the record."

"Record?"

"Sure," Harold said. "We keep a record of all the materials that come and go from the library."

"Can we see it?" Annie asked.

"Of course. It might take me a moment to find it, though. We keep those older documents in storage." While Harold was gone, Annie stamped her hand with one of the rubber stamps on the desk. *Overdue.* Natalie begged her to put the stamp back before anyone saw. Annie did — right after she gleefully stamped Natalie's hand. *Overdue.*

In a few minutes, Harold came back carrying a dusty leather folder. He showed them to a reading table near the drinking fountain. "Do you have clean hands?" he asked.

Annie inspected hers, which had mysterious blue stains on the palms. "Olive can turn the pages," she said.

"Okay. Call if you need me." Harold returned to the front desk.

The pages inside the leather folder were loose and yellowed, with curly old-fashioned handwriting. The top page said:

Materials considered inappropriate for children by the Doty Morality Society

Removed by community petition from Doty County Library September 1945

"What a lot of big, boring words," Annie said.

"It just means that a group of people wanted certain books to be kicked out of the library," Natalie translated. "This morality society petitioned for it, which means they collected signatures from the people who agreed with them."

"Like voting," Annie said.

"Yeah, like voting. Then they brought the list of signatures to the librarian and asked for the comics to be removed."

"But why would the librarian do it?" Annie wondered. "Librarians are the bosses of the books."

"This is a public library," Natalie said. "The books belong to everyone. If enough people want certain books — or comics — to go away, I guess the library has to remove them."

Natalie ran a clean finger down the long list of banned comic books. She turned page after fragile page, not finding a single mention of

Zadie. But on the very last page, in faded ink, was written:

The Adventures of Zadie Zeolite, Volumes 1–9

"Look at that!" Annie yelled, pumping her fist in the air. "Woo-hoo!"

"*Shhhh!*" said a woman standing near the law books. "Inside voice."

Natalie grabbed a tiny library pencil and blank slip of paper off the table. She scribbled, *Woo-hoo! Zadie was in this library!*

Annie wrote: *Aren't we great detectives?*

Natalie: *I wish there were pictures of Zadie in here to show Emily.*

Annie: *Me too. But let's go tell her what we discovered anyway!*

Chapter Thirteen

Natalie and Annie went straight to the Warsaws' house, excited to share their discoveries about Zadie Zeolite. But when they rang the doorbell, no one answered. So they returned to the Warsaws' the next day, Saturday, first thing in the morning.

This time when they rang the bell, Mr. Warsaw came to the door in a brown suit jacket and freshly ironed pants.

"Oh, girls!" he said, sounding surprised. "I was expecting someone else. He's due any minute."

"We have something exciting to tell you," Natalie said. "But should we come back later?"

Mr. Warsaw glanced anxiously at his watch.

"Actually, would you mind looking after Emily when Paul arrives?"

"No problem," said Annie. "Hi, Emily."

Mrs. Warsaw waved from the living room couch with a French cruller doughnut in her hand.

Mr. Warsaw straightened his suit jacket. "Help yourself to a doughnut."

Before he was done saying "doughnut," Annie had shot through the door. Leaning over the bakery box on the coffee table, she prodded several doughnuts before choosing one with chocolate sprinkles.

"Detectives like doughnuts," said Annie. "Even more than cops do."

Natalie helped herself to a cinnamon-dusted doughnut. "This kind looks good."

"It is," said Mrs. Warsaw. "I've had two of those already."

"Leave some for Paul, sugar pie," said Mr. Warsaw.

"Paul who?" asked Annie.

The doorbell rang, and Mr. Warsaw hurried to the

door. "Would you please take Emily upstairs now?" he asked Natalie. "I don't want Paul to upset her."

Through the front window, Natalie saw a man in a crisp black suit waiting at the door. He smiled pleasantly at her and seemed nice enough. Why would he upset Mrs. Warsaw?

"Yes, let's go upstairs," said Mrs. Warsaw. "I have a secret to show you in my bedroom closet." She rubbed her hands together mischievously.

Mr. Warsaw unlatched the door. "You must be Paul," he said. "Thanks for coming."

When Mrs. Warsaw, Natalie, and Annie reached the top of the stairs, Annie whispered, "Who is that man?"

Mrs. Warsaw shook her head stubbornly. "He can't hear the secret. It's only for us girls."

"We have a secret for you, too," Natalie said, hoping to distract Mrs. Warsaw from her pattern of looking for Zadie. Natalie couldn't bear to see her cry again. But Mrs. Warsaw paid no attention — she determinedly led the girls to her bedroom. Same as before, she insisted they open the closet and shove the clothes aside in search of Zadie.

"Feel along the back wall," Mrs. Warsaw said. "There's a secret panel. Zadie is behind it."

"A secret panel?" Annie said. "You didn't say that before."

Natalie stepped into the closet to have a look. "In any case, there's no panel here."

Just like last time, Mrs. Warsaw had to check for herself. And just like before, things ended with Mrs. Warsaw crying on her bed. "I'm not crazy. I know she's there," she said, her face pressed to a ruffled pillow. "Zadie."

"Zadie Zeolite," Annie said softly.

Mrs. Warsaw turned her tear-stained face to one side. "*Zeolite.* That's her last name. I forgot."

"We know that Zadie is real," Natalie said. "We discovered a list of comic books banned from the library when you were a girl. *The Adventures of Zadie Zeolite* was one of them. That's what we came here to tell you, Emily."

"*The Adventures of Zadie Zeolite.* Yes, that's right." A

distant look came over the old woman's heavily creased face. "Mother threw the other comic books away, but I saved Zadie."

"Did your mom work at the library?" asked Natalie.

"*Shhhh.*" Mrs. Warsaw closed the door with the toe of her tennis shoe. "No. She belongs to a society of ladies who don't like comics. They forced the library to throw them all away, because they think they're bad for us kids. But Zadie's not bad — she's wonderful. I saved her from the trash pile and hid her behind the secret panel in my closet. Mother doesn't know. Don't tell her!"

"We won't," said Natalie. "Do you remember where else you might've hidden the Zadie comics? Maybe you only thought you put them in your closet."

"I'm *sure* I hid Zadie in the closet." Mrs. Warsaw shut her eyes. "If I don't see her soon, I'm afraid I'll forget what she looks like. And if I forget that . . ." Mrs. Warsaw's voice trailed off into tears.

"Olive," Annie said, "gimme your notebook and pencil."

Annie sat on the carpet, balancing Natalie's note-book on her knees. "Zadie's tall, so I'm going to use the whole paper. She's flying toward a volcano, to the stream where she was born. See, Emily?"

The old woman sat up to watch Annie's drawing take shape. "She has hair down to her rear," Mrs. Warsaw said. "Don't leave that out."

"I won't." The side of Annie's hand whooshed against the paper as she penciled in flowing hair lines.

Mrs. Warsaw peered over the edge of the bed. "You forgot Zadie's crystal necklace. It's shaped like a heart. Her unitard has long sleeves. Now, draw her high-heel boots."

"How's this?" Annie held up the paper for approval.

"Yes. That's Zadie!" Mrs. Warsaw marveled at the drawing for a few moments, then eased her feet to the floor. Extending her arms, she began scuffing around the room in her tennis shoes. "Look, I'm flying." Natalie felt so proud of Annie and the pic-ture she had drawn to make Mrs. Warsaw happy.

After a couple of laps, Mrs. Warsaw said, "Why aren't you flying, too?"

Natalie and Annie flew around the two beds, their arms held out like airplane wings. Mrs. Warsaw shook her head in an attempt to make her wispy hair stream out behind her, like Zadie's hair.

"Zip! Zap! Zadie!" she cried.

"I'm high above the city," Annie said. "I can see the roofs of our houses."

"I'm even higher than you. I see London! I see France!" Mrs. Warsaw sang out, which made them all laugh.

Nobody noticed that Mr. Warsaw had opened the bedroom door and was watching them, until he spread his arms and said, "Emily! Fly to me." Mrs. Warsaw sailed happily into his embrace.

"I saw Zadie," she said.

"Paul's gone now," he told her, then turned to Natalie and Annie. "Thanks for watching my girl."

"It was fun," Natalie said, and Annie nodded.

Mr. Warsaw swayed with Mrs. Warsaw in his arms, slow dancing in place. He looked over her shoulder at the details of the room as if seeing them for the first time. "A lot of good memories in this house," he said. He took Mrs. Warsaw out into the hall. "We picked out this wallpaper together when we first got married. I refinished this banister." They walked down the stairs.

"This is my house," Mrs. Warsaw insisted. "It isn't fair!"

"I didn't want to sell the house, sweetheart, but I told you why we have to," Mr. Warsaw said. "You need that new treatment. The doctor said it could help your memory a lot, but it also costs a lot. We can't afford to stay here anymore."

Mrs. Warsaw rested her hand on a brass light switch. "I don't want to leave."

"I don't, either. But Paul's a good realtor. He promised us a good price on the house."

"You're moving?" Annie said in disbelief.

Natalie looked out the front window. Newly staked in the front lawn was a big white sign that said, *FOR SALE.*

162

Chapter Fourteen

Annie and Natalie sat in their office headquarters, drinking orange soda to shoo away the sadness about the Warsaws and their house.

Natalie hissed open her can and took a quiet sip. "I feel stupid," she said.

"Why?"

"Because I thought our investigation of Zadie was important." Natalie twanged the pop top, making a dull sound. "But they have much bigger things to worry about than superheroes, like Mrs. Warsaw's expensive medicine and losing their house. Compared to that, our investigation is useless."

"Not necessarily," Annie said, and took a deep swig. "You never know."

"If Emily actually had some Zadie comics hidden in her closet, the money they'd be worth would come in handy now." Natalie opened her notebook and scratched out a multiplication problem. "There were nine issues of *The Adventures of Zadie Zeolite* banned from the library, right?"

"Yep."

"And Derek said that one Zadie comic might sell for . . ."

"One hundred thousand dollars."

Natalie didn't need the notebook to solve that one. "Nine hundred thousand bucks. Almost a million dollars."

"That's a lot of money," Annie said. "Enough to buy plenty of fancy medicine. Enough to save the Warsaws' house! All we have to do is find them."

Natalie sighed. "Yeah. But there's no point in getting excited. Mrs. Warsaw's comics could be anywhere, if they even exist. Face it: We've hit a dead end."

"On *The Arthur Milligan Mysteries*, Miss Dimesworth and Agent Milligan *always* hit a dead end. It's an important part of the show. But no matter what, they always solve the case by the end. We'll find those comics somehow, I'm sure of it." Annie took another gulp of her soda. "*Ahhhh.* My mom loves orange soda, same as me."

Natalie matched Annie's swig, which made carbonation rocket up her nose. "Ow," she said, rubbing her forehead. "Any news from your mom?"

"It's too soon," Annie said. "It takes a while for letters to get to California. Good thing, or I wouldn't have time to plan things out." Annie snapped the pop top off her can and used it to etch a large square in the dirt floor. "This is the upstairs of my old house, see? I'll have my old room, and my mom can have Ralph's room here. And this third bedroom, which Charla used as a junk room, will be an art studio."

"Does your mom like art as much as you?"

Annie smiled. "Yep. She's the one who taught me to draw." Annie sketched in the bathroom and the stairs. "She could teach you, too. Want to learn?"

"Yes!" Natalie had always wished she could draw as well as Annie.

"We could have a pottery corner over here, and there should be a painting table, too. This right here is a hot-glue gun station. You can come over whenever you want to use it."

"Cool," Natalie said, kneeling on the edge of Annie's dirt-picture. "We could have sleepovers where we stay up all night and make art."

"You bet," Annie said. "My mom doesn't tell anyone when to go to bed."

Natalie raised her soda can. "To all-night sleepovers at your house."

Annie thunked her can against Natalie's. "To my mom."

TWEET!

The whistle blow outside was followed by a sharp kick on the wooden porch foundation. "I know you're in there! Come out with your hands up."

"Noah, leave us alone," said Natalie.

"I'm counting to three. One . . ."

"I'm staying right here," Natalie whispered.

". . . two . . ."

"He kicked my house," Annie muttered, "so I'm going to kick his butt. Come watch."

". . . three!"

As the girls crawled outside, Noah jerked his ticket pad from his tight back pocket. "This is your second one," he said, scribbling furiously. He shoved the pink piece of paper at Natalie as she got to her feet.

"'Ticket from the Law Club: For not being able to read,'" Natalie said. "But I just read this."

"Yeah, but you missed the sign on the front of the house," Noah said.

Annie jogged up the cement stairs of her old house, and stood beneath a bright red paper taped to the empty door frame.

"'Property condemned,'" she read, and turned to Natalie. "Condemned?"

"That means the house isn't safe to live in," Natalie said. She read the smaller print. "'Joe Quincy, City Inspector, has deemed this residence structurally unstable. Demolition November first.'"

"That's soon," Annie said. "Halloween is just a few days away."

"Yep," said Noah. "This old pile of Popsicle sticks is coming down."

Annie charged at Noah, who toppled backward onto the grass before Annie could even touch him. "Have some *respect!*" she shouted.

"You're an animal," Noah growled. "I can't believe I ever liked you. I can't believe you have even one single friend."

Annie's breathing was shallow and fast. Her eyes were on fire.

"Leave Annie alone, Noah," said Natalie. "Unless you want her to tell everyone your big fat secret."

Noah stood slowly, one stiff leg at a time. "Watch it," he said in a tone that meant business. "You already have two tickets. One more, and you win yourselves a ride in the squad car to jail."

"What squad car?" Natalie asked.

"This one." Noah blew three short bursts into his whistle. Something emerged from behind the Warsaws' hedge.

It was Ricky Wallis, Natalie's six-year-old brother. He ran toward them while holding a cardboard box up around his middle, like a big square skirt. Headlights were drawn on the front in blue marker, and what seemed to be jar lids clattered on the sides. The jar-lid wheels didn't turn because the squad car didn't touch the ground. It was powered purely by Ricky's short, sprinting legs.

"I'm coming!" he cried.

There was no top to the car, so technically it was a convertible. Duct-taped to both sides were flashlights covered in red and blue tissue paper.

"Deputy, turn on the flashers!" Noah demanded.

Ricky switched on the flashlights. The red and blue tissue paper glowed.

"What have you done to my brother?" Natalie said.

"I appointed him deputy of the Law Club. And the head builder. He made the squad car, and soon he'll finish the jail."

So *that's* why Ricky had been hammering boards together out by the garage. Natalie crossed her arms.

"Ricky, Noah is using you for his evil purposes. Go home."

Ricky parked the squad car, which amounted to leaning against a tree. "Noah plays with me. You don't."

"See? It's his choice." Noah put a hand on Ricky's shoulder. "But remember, Deputy, we're not playing. This is real."

Ricky nodded. "Need a ride, Sheriff?"

"Yes, but scoot over. I'm driving." Noah opened the flimsy cardboard door and walked inside the car. "Excuse me, criminals."

Noah slammed the door, which shook the entire car. He grabbed the construction-paper steering wheel. Taking tiny steps, he and Ricky turned the car around. Then Noah chanted, "Left . . . left . . . left, right, left," as he and Ricky marched off in their cardboard convertible squad car.

"For the love of dogs," Natalie said under her breath. But Annie wasn't beside her to hear the catchphrase. She was on the steps of her old house, staring up at the notice from the city.

"This house can't be torn down," Annie said.

Natalie leaned against the metal railing, which wobbled. "If the city is demolishing it so soon, the house must be in really bad shape. It could be dangerous to live here with your mom."

"It *can't* be torn down." Annie slapped the notice off the door frame and crumpled it into a ball.

"Elvis, you can't do that."

"I just did," Annie said. She stared intently at the balled-up notice, as if her eyes might have the superpowers to make it disappear. But they didn't, so Annie chucked the paper into the dead hydrangea bushes instead.

Chapter Fifteen

During fifth-period English, Missy Reynolds passed Natalie a folded note.

I'm riding the bus home with you today.

Natalie wrote back. *You are? Why?*

You'll see! Missy signed the note with a smiley face.

The whole bus ride home, Missy wouldn't tell Natalie what was going on. Whenever Natalie asked her questions, Missy just smiled mysteriously and shrugged her shoulders. *What is this all about?* Natalie wondered.

Natalie pulled her house key from her pocket, but she didn't need to use it — her mom was waiting on the porch, smiling the same mysterious smile as Missy.

"Mom, what's going on?"

"Surprise!" she said. "Welcome to your speech-writing party. Here, have a thinking cap." She handed Natalie and Missy each a paper party hat.

"Speech-writing party?" asked Natalie.

"It was Missy's idea. She knew you weren't excited about working on your campaign speech. So she called me when you were out with Annie and asked if I would help her make a party for you. It'll be easier to think of ideas while you eat cake." Natalie's mom clasped her hands anxiously. "Surprise?"

Missy and her mom looked so hopeful that Natalie would like the idea. Natalie didn't love surprises — especially after the business with Annie on the bus. But on the other hand, time was running out to prepare a speech. Natalie couldn't put it off anymore — the school assembly was in just a couple of days.

After a tense minute, Natalie strapped on her party hat. Missy and her mom cheered.

The dining room was decorated with the purple tablecloth the Wallises always used for birthdays. Streamers hung from the chandelier. A few sheets of white paper, a new pencil, a party blower, and a muffin paper filled with trail mix sat at each of the two place settings. In the center of the table, a chocolate cake — identical to a birthday cake — waited on the special silver party platter, the one that had belonged to Great-Grandma Wallis.

"Fun!" said Missy. She gently uncurled her party blower with her fingers. "Thanks for doing this, Mrs. Wallis. Natalie, it's just like your birthday last February."

"Was that the last time you were over?" Natalie's mom said. "It's been too long."

Natalie's mom invited them to sit down. She gave them each a champagne glass filled with sparkling ginger ale — the kind from the health food store. She cut thick slices of chocolate cake.

"This is so fancy," said Natalie.

Natalie's mom kissed Natalie's cheek. "Glad you

like it, sweetheart." She surveyed the table, then said, "Okay. I'll leave you ladies to your work." She took a plate of cake for Ricky and went out the back door, where Ricky was pounding nails.

Missy spread her napkin across her lap. Natalie decided she should, too.

"What do you have for your speech so far?" asked Missy, taking a dainty sip of ginger ale.

"Not one word."

"Don't worry," said Missy. "My dad has to write speeches all the time for City Council, so I know how they're supposed to sound." She lifted the frosting off her cake in one long strip and set it aside. "Let's eat first, and then we can start writing."

Before long, the doorbell rang. When Natalie opened the door she found Annie standing there in her choir robe.

"Today," Annie announced, "we are going to have a ceremony in honor of my old house and our headquarters."

"I can't," said Natalie.

"Olive, the house is going to be knocked down soon. We have to say our good-byes before it's too late."

"I *can't* today. I have a guest."

"What guest?" Annie stepped inside and took in the dining room scene. "It's your birthday and you didn't invite *me*?" She looked wounded.

"It's not my birthday. My mom invited Missy over to help me write my campaign speech. She made it like a party so the writing wouldn't seem so hard. That's all."

"Oh, what a great idea!" Annie said with relief. "Your mom is one smart lady." She picked up Missy's party blower, wailed into it for two seconds, then tossed it back on the table. Missy shrank from the used blower and Annie as if both were poisonous.

Natalie stepped between them. "Annie Beckett, this is Missy Reynolds. Missy goes to my school."

"I've known Natalie since first grade," said Missy. "I'm her campaign manager."

Annie shrugged. "That used to be my job."

"Wait," said Missy. "Are you the girl who handed out bags of old cookies on Natalie's bus?"

"Yep. Every bag had something unique in it," said Annie. "Unique like Natalie."

Missy had a bite of cake. "All I know is that someone broke their braces on a rock-hard cookie."

"Those cookies were more for decoration than eating," said Annie, sliding into a chair. "Can I have some cake?"

Natalie passed Annie her slice and her glass of ginger ale, too. She was less and less hungry every minute.

"Let's start writing," said Missy. "My dad is picking me up at six."

"Yeah, let's start," said Annie, her teeth covered in chocolate frosting.

Missy straightened her stack of paper. "My dad always begins his speeches with a quote by someone. A poet or a president."

Natalie rolled her pencil on the table. "I can't think of any quotes."

"I know one." Annie cleared her throat and sang, *"Who's got the crunch that makes you wanna munch? Reggie's Ruffle Chips! With dip!"*

Missy scoffed. "That's a song from a TV commercial, not a quote. We'll use the 'Four score and seven years ago' quote by Abraham Lincoln. That's always a good one." She wrote slowly in neat rows. "'. . . our fathers brought forth . . . conceived in liberty . . . all men are created equal.'"

"Olive isn't a man," Annie said.

Missy looked up. "What?"

"You said 'all men.'" Annie pointed her fork at Natalie. "*She* is a girl. Believe me, it's no fun being called a boy when you aren't one."

"I *know* she's a girl," Missy said. "So what? You want me to change President Lincoln's speech?"

"Why not?" Annie said. "He made it up. We can make up stuff, too."

"Abraham Lincoln was a *president*. His speech is *famous*. He did not 'make it up.'"

"Of course he did," said Annie. "Instead of saying the four-score stuff, he could've done a magic trick with that big hat of his. Or if they had Reggie's Ruffle Chips back then, he could've talked about how the burned ones taste the best."

"Excuse me?" Missy said.

"Everything is made-up." Annie tapped her plate for emphasis. "The idea that we should go to school — someone made that up. The ABCs: made-up. Words: made-up. So is your name. Your parents could've called you Penelope instead of Missy. Right, Olive?"

Missy turned to Natalie. "What is she talking about? And who's Olive?"

Natalie nudged Annie under the table, as a signal to stop making a scene. Apparently, Annie interpreted this as a cue to jump to her feet and grab Natalie's party blower.

"I'll show you what I mean, Missy," Annie said. "Watch."

Standing in the hallway, her dirty socks peeping from beneath her choir robe, Annie began singing.

"Cake is so great
You might want to marry it

179

So take it on a date
Or a ride in a chariot!"

Annie marched around the table in a one-person parade, hooting on the party blower.

"Go to a church, get married
To your tasty, tasty cake
When you die, get buried
Beside your poor, dead caaaake!"

Missy gave Natalie a long look that asked, *This person is your friend?* When the song ended after what felt like an eternity, Missy spoke first.

"Who wrote that?"

"Elvis."

"Elvis Presley wrote a song about cake?" Missy asked doubtfully.

"Not *that* Elvis. This one." Annie jabbed herself proudly in the chest. "I made it up just now."

"*Anyway*," Missy said. "After Lincoln's quote, you should give a statistic. Those are important. Like,

'Ninety percent of the student body prefers blue pencils to red pencils.'"

"But I don't know any statistics like that," said Natalie.

"You can fill in that part later. Next, tell people why they should vote for you." Missy held her pencil above the paper, at the ready. "So, why should they?"

"Because I really want to run the School Store," Natalie said. "It's my dream. And I think I'd be good at it."

"You can't say it plain like that. You have to say it fancy: 'My dear students, teachers, and staff. It is my supreme wish to become Student Council Secretary. Grant me this, and I will be faithful to *your* wishes.'"

"*Pffff.*" Annie didn't look up from the sketch she was making of the half-eaten cake. "Nobody actually talks like that."

"Important people do," said Missy. "Like my dad."

"Olive doesn't, and she's *very* important. As long as she speaks her mind, who cares if it sounds fancy or not? Isn't being yourself enough?"

Missy actually turned her chair to face Natalie, making it clear who she was *not* paying attention to. "A good speech is your best chance of winning." She handed Natalie the paper she'd written. "It's simple: Just read this."

Natalie folded the paper in half. True, Missy's speech was dull. It was drab. It was deeply, deeply boring. But it was safe. And just a few days shy of the school assembly, safe felt good. "I will read it," Natalie said. "Thanks."

Soon, Missy's dad came to take her home. Natalie said good-bye while Annie finished her cake drawing at the dining room table. When Natalie came back into the dining room, Annie handed her the drawing, which she had signed with big loopy letters.

"Did I ruin your party?" Annie asked with a look of great concern. "I was trying to help."

"I know," Natalie said. "And no, you didn't ruin anything. At least I have a speech to give now. I just hope I can do it without fainting."

Chapter Sixteen

O n the day of Natalie's speech, Annie stopped by before school. She opened her jacket to reveal a shirt full of Natalie's square campaign buttons.

"For good luck," said Annie. "Even though you don't need it. You practiced your speech a hundred million times."

Missy had come over again to coach Natalie on how to deliver the speech. Some parts should be loud, some soft, and she should always pronounce her Ts like English people. Missy had choreographed some hand gestures, too, to emphasize the most important parts. They worked on a special ending, which involved Natalie clasping her hands and giving thankful nods to the audience.

"Practicing yesterday made me less nervous," Natalie said. "But now the nerves are back. I tried, but I couldn't memorize the words."

"You'll do great," Annie said. "Just be yourself."

"Thanks, Elvis." Natalie picked up one of the paper buttons, which had fallen from Annie's shirt to the floor. "You're not wearing those to your school, are you? No one knows who I am."

"So? I know who you are," Annie said, and taped the button back onto her chest.

The lights on the auditorium stage were bright and hot, which made Natalie sweat from the moment she sat in her folding chair. Clara Winkle, also running for secretary, giggled nervously in the chair next to Natalie. Steven sat beside Clara, looking cool and calm. Trina George posed on a chair on the other side of the podium, her golden hair blow-dried into gleaming ripples. She waved to her friends in the back row as if she had already won the election.

The lights shining in Natalie's eyes made it hard to see individual faces in the dark auditorium. But she knew they were out there — everyone in the whole school — because she could hear them fidgeting in their seats as they waited for the assembly to begin. Missy was out there somewhere with a copy of the speech, ready to follow along and check if Natalie missed any words. Natalie clutched her own folded copy of the speech with both hands, like it was the edge of a steep cliff.

"Hello? Can you hear me?" Principal Tangleton tapped the microphone with her stout fingers. "Welcome, Newton Academy students. I hope you're ready to hear some great speeches from our Student Council candidates."

The audience applauded, and Natalie shrank at the sound of hundreds of pairs of hands clapping. It meant that hundreds of people were out there, and in a few minutes, she would have to speak to them. Natalie's forehead was sweating. Was it the lights, or was she developing a fever? *Calm down*, she told herself.

All you have to do is what you rehearsed. Just read the speech. She smoothed the folded paper against her leg.

The presidential candidates went first. When the principal called Trina's name, the whole back row went wild with applause — high-pitched screams from the girls and deep-throated bellows from the boys. Trina strolled to the podium, in no rush for this adoration to end. She took her sweet time adjusting the microphone to the height of her glossy lips.

"Good afternoon students, teachers, and staff. I'm Trina George. Thank you for coming to hear me speak today. If you've already promised me your vote, thank you. You've made the right choice. If you're still undecided" — a ripple of boos passed through the back of the auditorium — "maybe it will help to learn a little about me. I was just cast in a made-for-TV movie. I've gone to Newton Academy for nine years, so I know what this school needs in a Student Council President. I know what the students want. I have the answers you're looking for, so vote for me. Thank you."

The applause was mighty as Trina returned to her folding chair. After the presidential candidates came the people running for vice president and treasurer. Natalie didn't listen to their speeches. She merely counted them, knowing that each one brought her closer to her turn at the microphone.

"Thank you, Joey," said Principal Tangleton, and paused for a pale round of applause. "Now, our candidates for Student Council Secretary. First we'll hear from Natalie Wallis."

Natalie rose from her folding chair even though every cell in her body screamed at her to stay put. Her heart knocked around loose in her chest, making her shirt buttons seem to vibrate. As Natalie approached the podium, the glare from the lights lessened and she could see the ocean of faces before her. *Don't think about them,* Natalie told herself. *Just read the speech. It will be okay.* She set the folded paper — limp now from her sweaty hands — on the podium. She unfolded it. Inside, she did not find her speech written in Missy's flawless penmanship.

She found Annie's drawing of cake. The only words on the paper were in the lower right corner: *XOXO Elvis.*

Oh, no, thought Natalie. *Please no.*

The papers must have gotten mixed up when she was organizing her backpack that morning. She was so nervous, she hadn't paid attention to which folded paper she had grabbed off her desk.

Natalie riffled the cake drawing to make sure the speech wasn't glued to the back with sweat. It wasn't. She stared at the cake and tried desperately to remember how her speech began, but she had no memory of even the first word. Though she had practiced it a dozen times with Missy, her mind was blank.

Wait, no it wasn't. Some words were coming back to her . . .

Go to a church, get married
To your tasty, tasty cake
When you die, get buried
Beside your poor, dead caaaake.

The lyrics of Annie's infernal cake song crowded out any chance of recalling the campaign speech. Natalie's face felt hot again, but this time she knew it was not the lights or a sudden fever. It was fury.

She was so mad at Annie, and her dumb cake drawing, and her dumb cake song, not to mention her horrible campaign favors, which had nothing to do with Natalie or Student Council. And Missy! How could she make such ridiculously dull buttons and posters and write her such a complicated yet meaning-less speech that was impossible to remember? She had trusted Annie and Missy with her wish of being a leader on Student Council, and they had let her down. Jerks!

"Natalie?" whispered Principal Tangleton. "You may begin."

Tears pooled in Natalie's eyes, blurring the cake drawing. The truth, Natalie realized, was that she had let herself down. Student Council was about taking charge and being a leader. But Natalie hadn't taken charge of anything. She had let Annie and Missy swoop in like superheroes to rescue her, and make all the campaign choices. They had been the leaders, not Natalie.

Now, standing before the entire school with no speech and no plan, it was too late to take charge. A tear fell onto the cake picture. So far, this was the worst moment of Natalie's life.

"Natalie?" Principal Tangleton was growing impatient and so were the audience members, shifting in their seats.

Then, like shiny coins clinking into the School Store money box, more words dropped into Natalie's head. Not speech words, but Annie's words from the other day. *Everything is made up*, she had said. And, *Isn't being yourself enough?*

Natalie looked out at the crowd and made a choice. If nobody was coming to her rescue, she would rescue herself. She would fight for her dream of being Student Council Secretary and make up a speech, right then and there. She would speak from her heart and trust that it would be enough. Natalie would act like the leader she wanted to be, starting . . . NOW.

"Hello," she said into the microphone. Her voice was louder than she expected. "My name is Natalie Wallis, and I am running for Student Council Secretary."

That wasn't so bad. Now what? Natalie looked at the cake picture for inspiration.

"You know," she said, "standing up here is not a piece of cake."

The audience murmured. Some people giggled.

"I'm so nervous, my ears are ringing. My glasses are fogging up because my face is sweating, which never happens. But it's worth feeling afraid, because I get a chance to tell you how much I want to be Student Council Secretary. I believe I have what it takes to do a great job. I don't have all the answers, like some people. But in my opinion, a good leader has something more important than answers: questions."

Natalie's voice wasn't shaking anymore. Suddenly, standing up there felt as right and good as a number-two pencil. As her eyes adjusted to the light, she could see individual faces out in the audience. They were paying attention.

"I believe a good leader listens more than she talks," Natalie said. "And asks more questions than gives answers. Questions like, how do you think we can improve the School Store?"

Natalie removed the microphone from the stand and carried it around to the front of the podium. "I'm really asking you," she said. "How can we improve the School Store together?" Natalie searched the crowd until she saw a raised hand. "Yes, you with the yellow shirt."

"More pencils with planets on them," the boy called out.

"More pencils with planets!" Natalie said. "Yes! What else?"

"Pencil sharpeners that hold the shavings," said a girl.

"Great idea!" Natalie said.

"Ladybug erasers," said another girl.

Natalie pumped her fist. "Right on! How about one more?"

"Peanuts," said a kindergartner in the first row.

"Peanuts!" Natalie cheered. "As Student Council Secretary, I will take all of your suggestions into consideration. I will keep asking you questions. And together, we will find the right answers for the Newton Academy School Store."

Principal Tangleton started a thick round of applause. The students joined in, but the loudest clapping came from behind the podium, from Steven Redding. The applause worked like helium, lifting Natalie a few inches off the ground, or so it seemed. Natalie floated back to her folding chair and sat down. *I did it*, she thought. *I made up a speech. It was a piece of cake!*

The principal called Steven to the podium. A wave of cheers washed over Natalie's applause. Like fish jumping from the surf, shouts rose from the crowd. "Steve-O!" a boy yelled, and a girl squealed, "All RIGHT!"

Steven leaned an elbow on the podium. "Hey. My name is Steven —"

More squealing.

Steven smiled and shook his head. "My name is Steven Redding, and I have just one thing to say: Vote for Natalie Wallis, my friend and the best choice for Student Council Secretary. That's it."

Steven's friends and fans kept cheering, even after he had left the podium. When he turned back to his chair, he gave Natalie a secret thumbs-up, close to his chest so only she could see it. And he smiled his heartbreakingly crooked smile at her.

This, she thought, *is the best moment of my life.*

Chapter Seventeen

"Congratulations!" said Annie. "You're the Student Council Secretary!"

"Not yet," said Natalie, leaning against the headquarters wall. "There's still the election on Monday." She had, however, borrowed a school supply catalog from Miss Vang in the main office and circled all the things she planned to order for the School Store. Just in case.

Annie lit the candle and set it in the dirt bordering the army blanket. "I wish I could've been there to see your speech. I bet you were brilliant. Did Missy freak out that you didn't read her speech?"

"I thought she might," Natalie said. "But instead,

she said I handled the situation like a pro. And she gave me this." Natalie passed Annie a sheet of notebook paper. In her perfect handwriting, Missy had written down every word of Natalie's improvised speech.

Annie read it, then grinned. "This is great. Olive, you won everyone over today. Winning the election is a sure thing."

"Maybe," Natalie said modestly, though she secretly agreed with Annie. "We'll just have to wait till next Monday."

Annie ran her hand across the warped wooden wall. "By Monday, this house will be gone."

"It's so strange," said Natalie. "It's probably not even safe to meet here anymore."

"Yeah." Annie's voice was husky.

"Weren't you going to have a farewell ceremony for the house?" Natalie asked. "Let's do it now."

"Good call, Olive." Annie dragged the wooden crate from the corner and dumped the contents onto the blanket. "This can be the altar."

Natalie tipped the crate on its side so the open part was facing them. "Let's put the candle inside."

They surrounded the candle with special things: Natalie made some paper flowers with the supplies in her backpack. Annie added an unopened can of orange soda and a scattering of cheese puffs. Then Annie cut out a little paper bird, in honor of the swear bird she'd buried in the headquarters floor. Natalie creased the bird's hips and knees so he could sit on the soda can.

"We are gathered here today," said Annie, "to say good-bye to a very loyal companion. Fourteen seventy-five was a good house to me. When I lived here, it let me draw on its walls without a single complaint."

Natalie clasped her hands, as if praying. "It let us use this space under the porch whenever we needed it."

"On rainy days, the headquarters kept us dry," said Annie. "There are no rats or raccoons here, and the worms mind their own business."

"I hope that there is a heaven for good houses," said Natalie. "There, none of your boards will be broken, and your paint will smell new."

"Amen." Annie patted a splintery board kindly. "It isn't supposed to be this way. I was going to live here with my mom."

"I know," Natalie said. "But maybe you can find another house nearby. One that has room under the porch for a new headquarters."

"We need to find a house soon," Annie said. "My mom could show up any day now."

"What do you mean?"

"I've been thinking: Maybe she hasn't written back yet because she wants to drive up here and surprise me." Annie's eyes got wide. "Or if she has enough money, she'll fly on a plane. Then she'll be here even faster!"

Natalie took a pinch of dirt from the floor and sprinkled it into her hand. "What if your mom wants to take you back to California with her?"

"I never thought of that." Annie chewed the inside of her cheek. "I wanted us to live on this block. I belong here."

Someone outside of the headquarters kicked one of the porch boards.

"What." *Kick.* "Did." *Kick.* "I." *Kick.* "Tell you?" Noah shouted. "No trespassing!"

Annie's brow became stormy. "Oh, that's it." She scrambled through the opening in the wall. Natalie blew out the altar candle and chased Annie outside.

"This is my house!" Annie screamed at Noah. "Get out!"

Noah jumped onto the front steps and gripped the shaky railing as if it were a shield. "It's not your house anymore. And in two days, it's going to be *nobody's* house. A tractor's going to trash it."

"GET OUT OF HERE!" Annie rattled the bars of the railing like a wild animal in a cage. Natalie had never seen her so angry.

Noah threw a ticket through the iron bars. "That's your third one. You're coming with me to jail."

Across the street on Natalie's lawn, Ricky stood beside his makeshift wooden jail, beating a twig against the crooked slats.

"I'm not going anywhere with you," Annie said. She tore the ticket to confetti and flung it at Noah.

"But what I *am* gonna do is tell the whole world your secret."

Noah made fists at his sides. "No."

"Oh, yes." Annie's face developed a sinister smile.

"Who told you?" Noah whined. "That was supposed to be private. Anyway, my mom says a lot of kids sleep with their jeans on."

"Oh," said Annie casually. "Is that the secret? Thanks. Now I know."

The reality of what Annie had just accomplished dawned on Noah's face. "You . . . you tricked me."

"You deserved it," said Natalie.

"Oh, now you're *both* going to jail." Noah lunged at Annie, but she leaped out of reach. Next, he grabbed Natalie's sleeve.

"Run, Olive!" said Annie.

Natalie twisted free from his clutches, and the girls sprinted down the block. The *fip-fip-fip* of Noah's jeans was just a few feet behind them.

"Over there!" Annie pointed to the Warsaws'

house, where Mr. Warsaw was coming down the front walk with a cardboard box.

"Help!" Natalie cried.

Mr. Warsaw set down the box. "What's the matter?"

"Our enemy is chasing us," Annie panted. "Can we wait in your porch until he leaves?"

"Go on upstairs," said Mr. Warsaw. "You can help Emily pack."

Noah slowed when he saw Natalie and Annie entering the porch. He wasn't about to chase them inside someone's private property.

"You can't run forever!" Noah shouted.

In the upstairs bedroom, Mrs. Warsaw was holding up two suits — one navy blue and one frosting pink — by the hangers.

"Hi, Emily," Natalie said. "Do you need help with that?"

"I can't decide which to keep and which to give away." Mrs. Warsaw held the suits so they faced each other, as if introducing two strangers.

"Keep the pink," Natalie said.

"I vote blue," Annie said.

"Put them both in the box, tootsie pie." Mr. Warsaw set an empty cardboard box on the bed. "Our new apartment will have small closets. We won't have room for all our old things."

Sadly, Mrs. Warsaw dropped the suits in the box labeled DONATE.

"We should probably get rid of some of our shoes, too," Mr. Warsaw said. "I don't need my work boots anymore."

"Has somebody bought the house already?" Natalie asked.

"No. But our Realtor, Paul, said we should be ready to move on short notice, in case the house suddenly sells."

Mrs. Warsaw bent to pick up a pair of high-heeled boots. "I'm not giving these away!" she said. "These are just like Zadie Zeolite's."

"Wow," Annie said. "Did you used to wear those?"

"She sure did, every time we went dancing,"

Mr. Warsaw said with pride. "All right, angel. Put those in the 'Keep' box in the hall."

When Mrs. Warsaw had left the room, her husband heaved an armful of clothes from the closet into the donation box. "This is hard for her," said Mr. Warsaw. "She's lived on this block her whole life. She can't imagine leaving."

"We can't imagine you leaving, either," Natalie said. "I wish we could've helped you save the house." If only there *were* valuable Zadie Zeolite comics in the bedroom closet, as Mrs. Warsaw always said. Wait. That gave Natalie an idea.

"Mr. Warsaw," she said, "could Annie and I check the other closets in the house?"

Annie snapped her fingers. "Of course!"

"Go ahead," Mr. Warsaw said.

Natalie and Annie hurried around the house, checking every closet for the secret panel Mrs. Warsaw had described. But the search came up empty. When the girls returned to the bedroom, Mrs. Warsaw stood with her hand on the crystal doorknob to the closet.

"This is my house," she said firmly. "My closet. I put Zadie here, and I'm not leaving."

"I know how you feel," Annie said.

Mr. Warsaw put his arm around his wife's small waist. "We have to move, sweet pea. We have no choice."

Watching Mrs. Warsaw's face crumple into crying was the worst. It made Natalie's heart crumple, too.

Chapter Eighteen

At dusk, the streetlamps buzzed on one after another, as if they were playing tag. Annie stepped into a pool of light.

"We failed," Annie said, ripping off her fake mustache. "We are terrible detectives."

Natalie sighed. "I know."

"Miss Dimesworth and Agent Milligan *never* fail. Not even when you think they might. By the closing credits, every case is solved."

They passed through a shadowy spot, where the light from the streetlamp didn't reach. "They were detectives on TV," Natalie said. "In real life, not every mystery gets solved. Some mysteries, like this one, have more questions than answers."

"Yeah," Annie said in an utterly dismal tone. "Well, there's nothing to do now but eat dinner. Come on."

"You're positive I'm invited?" Natalie said. "You asked first?"

"Olive, you're *invited*."

Annie unlocked the back door, and a warm cheese smell welcomed them inside. "Hi, Grandma Hatch."

"Hi, firefly." Ms. Hatch turned from the stove. "And Natalie!" She sounded glad to see her, but a little too surprised.

"Can Natalie stay for dinner?" Annie asked.

"Of course!" said Ms. Hatch.

"Thank you," Natalie said, then she shot Annie a look. "And thank *you* for asking first."

Annie slumped into a chair at the kitchen table. "What's the difference? She'd say yes either way."

"That's true, Natalie. So who did the E & O Detective Agency help today?" Ms. Hatch said over the sound of chopping vegetables.

Annie put her head on the table. "Absolutely no one."

"We tried to help the Warsaws, but we weren't successful," Natalie said. "They have to sell their house to pay for Mrs. Warsaw's medicine."

The knife was silent on the cutting board. "Poor Emily. All of her memory troubles, and now she's losing both of her houses."

"Both of her houses? What do you mean?" asked Annie.

"She's selling the house where she lives now," Ms. Hatch said. "And the house she grew up in is being demolished in a couple days."

"But that means . . ."

"That Emily grew up in the house where you lived with your uncle." Ms. Hatch swept the carrots and tomatoes off the cutting board and into the salad bowl. "She's lived on this block her whole life."

"Mr. Warsaw mentioned that," said Natalie. "But I thought he meant that she lived in the same house, where they are now."

"No." Ms. Hatch dished salad and macaroni onto three plates. "She lived next door to me until she got married. When I was about your age, I used to spy on her from my bedroom as she got ready for her dates. I loved seeing Emily put on makeup and her pretty pearl earrings and a twirly skirt . . ."

"Hold on. You lived here when you were my age?" Annie said. "How come you never told me that?"

"You never asked," said Ms. Hatch with a friendly shrug. "This was my parents' house. I moved away to college and lived in New York City for a few years, but I moved back when my dad got sick."

"Which bedroom was yours?" Annie asked.

"The one you have now," Ms. Hatch said. "Let's sit down and eat."

"Which bedroom was Emily's?"

"The one at the back of the house, facing us."

"But that was my bedroom, too!" said Annie. She stared down into her macaroni. "This is really blowing my mind."

"Do you need a tissue, dear?" asked Ms. Hatch.

"No, just the pepper." Lost in thought, Annie peppered her plate with slow-motion shakes.

"Let me get this straight," Natalie said. "Mrs. Warsaw lived next door and had Annie's old bedroom. And Annie's old window. And *Annie's old closet*."

Annie looked up from her macaroni, which was dark gray from all the pepper. "My closet," she whispered. An electric current of understanding zip-zapped between the girls.

"Yes," said Ms. Hatch. "Funny to remember those days gone by. Do you want dessert?"

"Yes, please," Annie said.

Ms. Hatch dug out two ice-cream sandwiches from the foggy freezer. She handed one to each girl, then poured out two cups of hot tea. "Good night, ladies. I'm going up to read before bed."

Natalie thanked Ms. Hatch for dinner, and said that next time she would call to *make sure* she was invited. Ms. Hatch said there was no need — she was always welcome.

When they heard the rocking chair creak upstairs,

Natalie said, "Elvis, your old closet! Do you remember if there's a panel in the back of it?"

"I didn't have any clothes good enough for hangers," said Annie, "so I didn't even *use* my closet. But what if there *is* a secret panel? And what if the comic books are behind it?" In her excitement, she dipped her ice-cream sandwich into her hot tea. A chunk broke off and sunk to the depths. "Oops. That was a bad move."

Natalie peeled back the cold, wet paper of her ice-cream sandwich. "If there was even one Zadie comic in the closet, it could help Mr. and Mrs. Warsaw."

"And if there were lots of Zadie comics," Annie said, "they could be almost-millionaires. They could buy a diamond ring for every finger."

"They don't need diamonds," Natalie said. "They just need the best medicine for Emily, and to be able to keep their house."

Annie drained her teacup, which involved eating the soggy sandwich cookie at the bottom. "We have to go to my old house now and see if the comics are there."

"We can't just waltz in the door," said Natalie. "It's private property."

Annie steepled her hands as Miss Dimesworth sometimes did on TV. "Olive, in two days the city is going to tear the house down. Soon, there's not even going to be a door to walk in. And our chance to help the Warsaws will be gone forever."

"Well, when you put it that way . . ."

"Goodie," said Annie. "Let's go tonight."

"Wait. If we're going to do this, we need a plan."

Annie gave her a blank look. "A plan?"

"Tomorrow is Halloween," Natalie said. "We'll disguise ourselves as trick-or-treaters to investigate your old house. No one will notice us walking around at night, because there will be lots of kids out in the dark."

"That's genius, Olive."

"Come to my house after dinner," said Natalie. "Wear a costume."

Chapter Nineteen

Ding-dong.

"Our first trick-or-treater!" Ricky Wallis raced around the living room in a plastic spaceman suit. Natalie's dad sat on the couch in a clown costume and red yarn wig, smearing white paint onto his cheeks.

"Can someone else answer it?" he said. "I'm still putting on my makeup."

"I will." Natalie ran to the door and opened it. There stood Annie wearing her blue choir robe, but that was only the beginning of her Halloween costume. She had safety-pinned plastic spider rings to the shoulders of the robe and wore what looked like all of Ms. Hatch's brassy bead necklaces. Fake blood trickled from the corners of her mouth, and a mustache made with fresh hair and tape clung lopsidedly to her upper lip. In one hand, Annie held a pillowcase and in the other, a soup ladle. She smiled, revealing a plastic set of fangs.

"What *are* you?" Natalie asked.

"A vampire witch pirate," Annie said. "I couldn't pick just one thing."

"What's with the ladle?"

Annie pulled her hand up into her sleeve, so only the ladle scoop was showing. "It's the closest thing Grandma Hatch had to a pirate hook." She clawed the air with it. "Where's *your* costume?"

Natalie unzipped her oversized winter coat to reveal a green flowered dress. "I'm an old-fashioned prairie girl. It's what I am every year."

"Did people wear puffy pink coats back in the prairie days?"

"No," Natalie said. "My mom is making me and Ricky wear our winter coats because it's so cold."

"I don't want my prairie girl or my spaceman getting sick, that's why," Natalie's mom said. She twirled to show off her patchwork clown dress. "It's the first really cold night of the season. To be fair, Dad and I will wear our coats, too."

"Wow! Nice costume, Mrs. Wallis."

"Thank you, Annie. I like yours, too. Are you a . . . zombie chef?"

"Close!" Annie said. "Vampire witch pirate."

Natalie's mom laughed. "That was my next guess."

"Let's head out," said Natalie, "before all the good candy is gone." She winked at Annie.

Mrs. Wallis kissed Natalie on the cheek, then Annie. "Have fun. Be safe."

Outside, Natalie asked Annie, "Did you bring your flashlight?"

"Shoot. I forgot."

"It's okay. I have mine." Natalie patted a lump in her jacket pocket. "But if we only have one flashlight, we should bring extra batteries. Just in case."

"Batteries? I have some right here in my pocket," said Annie. "Let's go."

During the daytime, Annie's old house looked defeated, like someone had punched its lights out for good. But at night, with the streetlamps reflected in the dark windows, the face of the house came alive again. Whenever a car drove past, the yellow window-eyes darted menacingly. The warped wooden siding cast sneering shadows on itself. Cold wind whistled through the missing porch door. The whole house seemed to say, *Come and get me. I am ready for you.*

"Ready to go in?" Annie asked.

Natalie stayed where she was on the crumbly front walk. Overhead, the last of the dry leaves rattled in the branches. "I have a bad feeling about this," she said.

"Let's do some trick-or-treating first, to warm up," said Annie. "Keep an eye out for houses where me and my mom could live."

"Okay," Natalie said, quickly turning away from the creepy old house.

"Hey, check this out." Annie called Natalie over to Albert's apple tree. Someone had stapled a piece of paper to the bark.

"Let me guess," Natalie said. "More laws."

"No. It's even better." Annie read the sign out loud.

WANTED

Annie Beckett & Natalie Wallis

Also nown as Elvis & Olive

Crime: Runing from the law

Note: The names Elvis & Olive have four of the same leters. When you put them together they spell EVIL.

Reward: Your choise of actshun figure — anyone but Aqua King

The bottom half of the poorly spelled poster was decorated with portraits that Natalie guessed were supposed to be her and Annie, though they barely looked human.

"Evil," said Natalie, shivering. "I never noticed that. The letters also spell 'vile.'"

Annie studied the poster. "They spell 'live,' too. Do you have a pencil?"

"Of course." Natalie pulled a pencil from her trick-or-treat bag — she had brought one just in case. Annie added *VILE* and *LIVE* to Noah's sign. Then she made some changes to Noah's portrait of her. "My hair is way spikier than he drew it. And now I have vampire teeth. There."

The girls made their way to Albert Castle's porch, which glowed purple from a Halloween light bulb. When they rang the bell and shouted "Trick or treat!" a shadowy shape rose from the bench in the corner of the porch. A chilling guitar chord drifted toward them.

"You have disturbed the . . . Ghost Musician!" Albert sang. Cotton cobwebs swayed from the neck of his guitar. A woman in a long white dress came from inside the house and dropped a pack of gum into each of their treat bags.

"A pioneer girl," she said, "and a . . . a . . ."

"Vampire witch pirate," Annie said.

The lady threw back her head and let loose a laugh that popped like popcorn and rolled like doughnuts.

"Are you Donna?" Annie asked.

Albert cleared his throat. "Elvis and Olive, I'd like you to meet my lady, Donna. She's also the lead singer of my new band, Donna and the Doughnuts."

"Very nice to meet you," said Natalie.

"*The* Elvis and Olive?" Donna asked. "Al, sing the song you wrote about them!"

Albert strummed the guitar strings nervously. "It's not finished yet, but . . . okay."

"E & O
Are in the know
Solving mysteries
Door to door
They're the E & O Detective Agency!
They'll help you with your problems, it's a guarantee
E and O, O and E
Ding-dong, who's there? Annie and Natalie!"

Annie clapped and did a happy dance. "We have our own theme song, just like *The Arthur Milligan Mysteries!*"

Virginia Brooks's porch was dark, but Annie ran up the front walk anyway.

Natalie caught her sleeve. "No, Elvis. A dark porch means 'Don't trick-or-treat here.'"

"Says who?"

"Everyone. It's the universal language of trick-or-treat." As they turned to leave, the porch light snapped on. The door creaked open and out stepped Ms. Brooks, dressed in a tan trench coat and a bouffant wig. Her lips and her nails were both painted a glossy beige.

"Miss Dimesworth!" Annie breathed.

Ms. Brooks strode out the door to the end of the sidewalk, did a turn, and walked back, like a runway model. "What do you think?"

"You're beautiful," Annie said.

"You told us you never wore the costume any-more," Natalie said. "What changed your mind?"

"You girls did." Ms. Brooks patted her hair. "You helped me remember that I still have some Miss Dimesworth in me. And see? The dress still fits."

"It sure does. Can I touch it for luck?" Annie asked. Ms. Brooks held out the tail of the fabric belt. Annie kissed it.

TWEET!

Across the street, Noah Redding stood in a puddle of light below the streetlamp. In addition to his whistle, he wore a black cowboy hat and a black vest with a silver badge glinting on his chest. And as always, he wore his midnight blue, skintight jeans.

"There they are," Noah announced. "The outlaws."

"Ha!" said Annie. "There ought to be a law against *you*."

Two of Noah's school friends ambled down Sergeant Dewey's front walk, puzzling over the energy bars the sergeant had just dropped in their treat bags. Both wearing cowboy hats like Noah's, the boys were apparently the newest Law Club recruits.

"There are the fugitives I was telling you about," Noah said. "If you catch them, you can have all my candy."

Noah didn't need to say it twice. The two boys shot across the street toward Natalie and Annie, their bags of candy shaking like maracas at their sides. Noah ran after them.

"I'll hold them off, girls!" Ms. Brooks said, hurrying down the front walk. She tossed a handful of Tootsie Pops into the air to distract Noah's friends. But it only worked for a moment.

"This way, Elvis," Natalie said. She picked up the hem of her prairie dress and ran as fast as she could. They wove in and out of their neighbors' yards and through the alley, trying to lose Noah and his posse. But the boys were never far behind.

"Over here," Annie said in a loud whisper. She darted through the chain-link fence of her old backyard. She and Natalie ran for the back door of the condemned house.

Natalie tried the door. "It's locked! They're coming."

Annie jerked the doorknob up and jiggled it hard. The latch clicked open and they slipped inside.

When their breathing was back to normal, Annie stole a look out the dusty curtains. "We lost them."

"How did you do that with the door?" Natalie asked.

Annie smiled. "I lived here, remember? Practically all the locks are broken like that. You need the magic touch to open them."

The kitchen was illuminated with a hint of light from Ms. Hatch's house next door. But the hallway ahead was as black as an unlucky cat. "I'm scared," said Natalie. "Maybe this wasn't a good idea."

"We'll only be here a few minutes," Annie said. "Do it for the Warsaws."

"Okay." Natalie clicked on her flashlight. A creak came from the rusty stove, splattered with old grease. "What if there are ghosts?"

"If there are, we should say hello." Annie waved both hands. "Hi, ghosts. What's shakin'? Your chains, you say?"

"Elvis! For the love of dogs."

"I'm just kidding," said Annie. "Gimme the flashlight."

Annie lit the way up the musty carpeted stairs. Natalie held tight to the back of Annie's choir robe until they were in Annie's old bedroom. The mural Annie had drawn on the plaster walls was still there. It included a lush forest, tall mountains, horses running through flowers, and a naked princess holding a wand.

"It's so weird to be in here again," Annie said, touching the wall.

"But you know what's *really* weird? This room is the same shape as the Warsaws' bedroom. Two windows over here, across from the door. And the closet, facing diagonal like that. No wonder Emily got confused."

Annie grabbed the knob of the closet door. "Ready to see if Zadie's really here?"

Fear squeezed Natalie's insides. "What if there's a ghost in there?"

Annie calmly swung her candy bag over her shoulder. "If there is, I will smack its face with my Halloween candy," she said.

"Me too." Natalie moved her treat bag into striking position and steadied the flashlight beam on the door. "I'm ready now."

Chapter Twenty

The hinges groaned as Annie opened the closet door. Natalie aimed the flashlight beam inside the small, dark space. The hanger bar was bare. An old bedsheet lay bunched in one corner. And halfway up the back wall was what looked like an empty white picture frame.

The secret panel Mrs. Warsaw had told them about. It was real.

"I lived here for months, and I never noticed that," Annie said. "I feel dumb."

"Let's open it," Natalie said, her ears ringing with fear and anticipation.

Annie tugged at the corners of the panel. "It's painted shut."

"Use your ladle to pry it open," Natalie suggested. Annie slipped the scoop under one of the edges and yanked. The panel popped off and fell to the floor with a loud clatter.

Annie let the dark hole swallow her arm to the elbow. "There's something in here," she said. She pulled out a single strap-on roller skate with rusty metal wheels. Next, she found a few red checkers.

"Nothing else?" Natalie asked, her hope wearing thin.

"Only this." Annie slid a wide shoe box out of the hole and set it on the floor, sending up a wheeze of dust. "See what's inside, Olive."

Natalie knelt to lift the cardboard lid. When she saw what was inside the box, she drew a shaky breath. "'The Adventures of Zadie Zeolite,'" she read from the cover of the comic book. Natalie touched it to confirm she wasn't dreaming.

Under the sweeping red title, Zadie flew in a purple unitard over a twinkling city, her long hair

226

streaming behind her like a copper flag. Her crystal necklace sparkled with rainbow prisms, and a jagged speech bubble contained the signature cry: "Zip! Zap! Zadie!"

"Wow," Natalie breathed.

Annie carefully lifted the comic book. "It looks like there are lots more underneath. The Warsaws will be SO RICH!" Annie shouted.

"*Shhhh!* Someone might hear you. This house is supposed to be empty, remember?" Natalie yanked the closet door shut to muffle Annie's shouts.

"Zip! Zap! Zadie! Yip, yap, woo-hoo!" Annie jumped up and down. "Come on, Olive, lemme hear a *woo-hoo*. No one can hear us with the door closed."

Natalie laughed. "Woo-hoo!"

"Let's make sure there really are more Zadies under the first issue," Annie said. She tugged the bunched-up bedsheet from the corner and smoothed one edge of it onto the floor. Gingerly, Natalie lifted *The Adventures of Zadie Zeolite, Volume One* and set it on the sheet.

"*Volume Two* is underneath!" Natalie cried.

One by one, Natalie removed the rest of the comic books from the box. All nine volumes were there, plus three duplicates, making twelve Zadie comics in all.

"Are you doing the math?" Annie asked.

"You bet," said Natalie. "Let's pack these up and get out of here." She returned *Volume Nine* to the box, then the two copies of *Volume Eight*. "Can you imagine the look on Emily's face when she sees these? She will be so happy."

Annie aimed the flashlight into the box. "Mr. Warsaw will be even happier, once he finds out how much these are worth." She put her foot on the roller skate and squeaked it back and forth.

"Point the light down here," said Natalie, "so I can see what I'm doing."

"I *am* pointing it at you," said Annie.

The flashlight winked a shade dimmer. "The batteries are running out. Pop in the spares."

Annie gave Natalie a disturbingly vacant look. "The spares?"

"The spare batteries, Elvis! You told me you had some in your pocket!"

"I was joking, obviously," Annie said. "Who walks around with pockets full of batteries?"

"Oh, for the love of . . ." Natalie placed the last comic book on top and closed the box. "Let's leave before the batteries die."

Annie turned the doorknob. "Uh-oh," she said. She held the flashlight under her armpit as she jiggled the knob with both hands. She jerked the door. She kicked it. "Olive, it won't budge."

Blood pounded in Natalie's ears. "Let me try," she said. Natalie rattled the heavy crystal knob as hard as she could. Too hard, apparently, because it fell off in her hand. "Oh, no!"

Annie shook her head. "What did I tell you? All the doors in this old place are busted."

"If you *knew* that, why didn't you warn me not to shut the closet door?"

"I was busy celebrating the comics!" Annie said. "I wasn't thinking about broken locks."

Natalie held her head and groaned. "This is not good."

"Don't worry," Annie said.

The last thing Natalie saw was Annie's reassuring smile. The flashlight faded and the closet went black.

In the dark, Annie tried every trick she knew to open sticky doors with broken latches. She tried to spring the lock from the inside with her pinkie. She stuck the ladle handle where the knob had been. She took a running start and slammed her shoulder into the door. When none of these things worked, Annie and Natalie shouted at the top of their lungs for help. But no one came.

Finally, they had to admit it. They were trapped.

It was cold in the closet, and Natalie and Annie shivered. The warmth they had felt after running from Noah was long gone.

"Elvis, come share my coat," said Natalie. Annie accepted the right sleeve and zipped up the front. It was a tight fit with both of them in the jacket, but it was warmer that way.

"I thought the shouting would work for sure," Annie said. "The trick-or-treaters should've heard us."

"It's late. Everyone's gone home."

"We have a superhero stuck in here with us, but she can't help," Annie said. "That would be funny if I wasn't so tired."

"Being stuck isn't even the worst part." Natalie's voice was somber. "The city demolition crew is coming here tomorrow at eight in the morning. If we're not out of here by then . . ."

"We'll be demolished, too," Annie said.

"Yeah." Natalie wiped her running nose on her coat sleeve.

"I bet your parents and Grandma Hatch are searching for us right now."

"Yes, but they won't look for us in here. Everyone thinks this house is empty," Natalie said, fighting back tears. "We didn't tell anyone where we were going."

"Okay," Annie said in a soothing tone. "Let's sit down."

With both girls wearing Natalie's coat, sitting required coordination. They leaned their backs against the wall for balance, then slid down to the ground with a thump.

"We finally solved this case and found what we need to help the Warsaws keep their house," Natalie said. "I actually have a chance of winning the Student Council elections on Monday. Just when things start to go good, how can they go so bad?"

"I know." Annie was quiet for a minute. "We sent that letter to my mom almost two weeks ago. I should've heard from her by now. Why isn't she writing back?"

"She said she needed to earn some money in order to come get you," Natalie said. "Maybe she has to work for a while."

"She should at least write back!" Annie's voice wobbled.

Natalie reached for Annie's sleeve and hugged her close. Since they were both wearing the coat, it felt strange, as if Natalie was hugging Annie and herself at the same time.

"Your mom said she loved you," Natalie reminded her.

"She *should* love me! That's supposed to be her main job," Annie said. "I want to see her again, just so I can tell her what a terrible mom and big jerk she is for running away. Watch, I'm going to get us out of here, Olive."

In the darkness, there was a rustling.

"Oh, no," said Natalie. "There's a mouse in here."

"It's just me. I'm unwrapping a piece of candy."

"How can you be hungry at a time like this?"

"Sugar helps me think. And we have to think of a way out." Annie's candy-filled pillowcase snagged on the coarse floorboards as Annie pushed it toward Natalie. "Have something."

Blindly, Natalie chose what she hoped was a Snickers and took a bite. More bad luck: It was a Baby Ruth.

After a minute of thoughtful chewing, Annie said, "I got an idea." She grabbed Natalie's hand in the darkness. "In your mind, shout out to every single person you know. Use your psychic powers to ask them to help us."

"Psychic powers?"

"You know you got 'em, Olive. Even more than me."

"I'll try," said Natalie.

Mom? Dad? Ricky? Silently, Natalie called each name like a question. *Ms. Brooks? Miss Dimesworth? Mr. and Mrs. Warsaw? Please help us. Albert? Harold? Sergeant Dewey? Steven? Steven? Please come help.*

"I'm so cold and tired," said Natalie. "I can't keep my eyes open anymore."

"Me neither." With her free hand, Annie spread the sheet on the floor. She tossed her pillowcase of candy to the top of it. "On the count of three, lie back," she said.

One, two, three, and they fell backward softly. Natalie nestled her head into the candy pillow, her skull pressing into what felt like a Blow Pop.

Natalie closed her eyes. She opened them again. It was so dark, there was no difference. Natalie would never see the School Store table laid out with gleaming, fragrant school supplies. She would never read another book, or write another word, or see the faces of her family again. This was the end.

"Elvis," Natalie said, "I'm so scared."

Annie grabbed her hand inside the coat. "Whatever happens, I'm here." There was a long pause. "There's no one I'd rather be trapped in a closet with more than you."

"Me neither," said Natalie. "Annie, you're my hero."

"Natalie, you have been *my* hero since the day I met you. And you always will be," Annie said. "Now, let's sleep."

When she couldn't fight it anymore, Natalie let her eyes drift closed.

She dreamed she was stuck in outer space with the cold darkness and pulsing stars. Earth was far below, a lost marble on a great stretch of blacktop. Natalie zoomed, superhero style, toward the blue-and-white swirled marble. She flew past the stars so swiftly, they all grew tails of light, like comets. The Earth quickly became the size of a jacks bouncy ball, then a four-square ball. It grew bigger and bigger as Natalie rushed toward it, until there was no more ball, only her own street.

The neighborhood was as silent as space, except for a deep rhythm like a giant heart beating. The darkness was replaced by daylight, and it grew brighter by the second until soon, a blaze much stronger than the sun shone down on Natalie.

This is the light that comes to get people when they die, Natalie realized. *I'm dead.*

Chapter Twenty-One

"I'm dead," Natalie mumbled.

"No, you're not, Olive. Wake up!" Annie shook her shoulder. "There are people in the house."

Natalie woke from her strange dream and listened to the voices downstairs. "I hear my dad," Natalie said. "DAD!"

"They're upstairs!" someone called, and a few sets of feet thumped up the stairs. Annie unzipped the coat and snaked out of her sleeve.

"We're in here." Annie pounded the door with her fist. "In the room with drawings on the wall."

"The bedroom closet!" cried Ms. Hatch, and the footsteps rushed closer. The knob rattled on the other side of the door.

"Dad, the latch is stuck," said Natalie.

"Girls, stand back," said a voice Natalie didn't recognize. Picking up the precious box of comics, Natalie hurried to the back wall of the closet. A man in a police uniform crashed the door open with his meaty shoulder. Natalie's mom and dad and Ms. Hatch stood behind him, frantic looks on their faces.

"Girls!" said Ms. Hatch, bursting into tears.

Annie ran to her. "Grandma!" She flung her arms around Ms. Hatch's broad back.

Natalie's mom kneeled to hug Natalie and sobbed. "We thought . . . we were afraid . . ."

"Natalie Marie," said her dad, his voice cracking. "What in the world are you doing in here?"

Natalie squeezed them both. She had never been so glad to see anyone.

"We didn't mean to get stuck, but —" Natalie began.

"Explain *later*," Natalie's mom said sternly. "The city demolition crew is waiting for us to leave so they can tear down this house."

In a daze, Natalie and Annie followed the adults down the stairs and out the front door. Close to a hundred people were gathered in the street in front of Annie's old house, and they cheered when Natalie and Annie emerged. The cold air turned everyone's breath to smoke.

Mixed in with the people she didn't recognize, Natalie found the familiar faces of her neighbors: Virginia Brooks, and Mr. and Mrs. Warsaw, and Albert Castle, and Sergeant Dewey, to name a few. Steven was there, too — *Steven!* — and a man sitting at the controls of a big yellow excavator looking both tired and irritated. Ricky ran out of the crowd and hugged Natalie around the waist.

"Nat, I was worried," he said.

She put her arms around him. "I'm okay, Rick."

"Olive," Annie said. "In your psychic message, how many people did you call for help?"

"Everyone I could think of."

"You're good," Annie said. She tapped the police officer on the elbow. "Did you get our psychic message, too?"

The officer pointed into the crowd. "That boy told us you were here."

Noah stepped forward looking meaner than he ever had before. "That's right, *Elvis* and *Olive*. I saw you go in that house, that *private property*, last night. When the police officer knocked on our door this morning and asked about you, I told him everything. You're in huge trouble and I'm glad! You can go to real jail now for all I care."

Annie ran to Noah. She grabbed his curly hair and pulled his face toward hers. She kissed him on the cheek.

Noah's face changed from a mask of wild anger to one of joyful shock.

"You saved our lives," Annie announced. "Noah Redding SAVED OUR LIVES!"

"Right on, hero," said Albert. "High five."

"*No-ah, No-ah,*" Ricky Wallis chanted. Mrs. Warsaw

joined in, then Ms. Brooks, and Steven Redding, and soon everyone was saying it.

Noah pointed at Annie. "You . . . kissed me."

"I feel like kissing the whole world," Annie said, throwing her arms open wide. "*Mwah!* We are alive!"

The police officer landed a huge hand on Noah's back. "Nice work, son." Noah looked up at the officer with undisguised awe.

"It's time to go home," said Natalie's dad. "Noah is right. You *are* in big trouble."

"I know," Natalie said. "But give me one more minute." Holding the dusty shoe box between them, Natalie and Annie wove through the group to where Mr. and Mrs. Warsaw stood huddled in an afghan blanket. "We went into the old house for you," Natalie explained, "to find these." She carefully lifted the box top.

Mrs. Warsaw gasped. "Zadie? Zadie Zeolite!" She held both hands over the colorful comic book cover, as if it was giving off heat. In disbelief, she touched Zadie's face with one finger.

"They were behind a panel in the closet, just like Emily kept telling us," said Natalie to Mr. Warsaw. "But her *old* closet in her *old* house."

"The house where she grew up," said Mr. Warsaw, nodding slowly. "Of course. You were telling the truth, sweet pea."

"I always do," Mrs. Warsaw said.

"I didn't understand. I'm so sorry."

Mrs. Warsaw clapped the lid back on the box. "If Mother sees these, she'll throw them in the trash!"

"My love," Mr. Warsaw said, "I promise that your mother will not throw anything away." He kissed her cheek.

"It's a good thing she won't," Annie said. "Those comics are worth enough to save your house and buy a truckload of medicine, too."

"I wish," Mr. Warsaw said, looking doubtfully into the shabby shoe box.

"Is Derek Takeda here?" Natalie shouted into the throng.

"Yeah," said a crabby voice nearby. "Not by choice." Derek pushed through the crowd, Millicent tappity-tapping behind him with Chicken at her side. "Millie wanted to see the house fall down and Mom and Dad insisted that we *all* go and of course the *dog* had to come and —" Derek stopped cold when he saw what was in the box. "Holy . . . are those what I think they are?"

"Yep," said Annie. "The full collection of Zadie Zeolite comics, plus a few extra copies."

"Whoa. Wow!"

"Derek," Natalie said, "would you explain to the Warsaws how much these are worth?"

"Of course. Oh my gosh, oh my gosh." Derek ran circles around himself, as Chicken always did, and Millicent tap-danced happily in her brother's wake. "First, you have to get them inside. It's *way* too cold out here. And you should put them in dust jackets, like, *yesterday*. If you're thinking about selling — wow — get ready to be rich."

"Rich?" Mr. Warsaw said hopefully.

Natalie and Annie grinned at each other.

"*Very* rich," Derek said. "I have all the selling supplies at my house. Mr. and Mrs. Warsaw, come with me." The Warsaws hurried to catch up with Derek, who was practically leaping down the street with excitement.

"I'm staying here with Mom and Dad and Chi-Chi," Millicent called after him. "We're going to watch the house get wrecked."

"Everybody out in the street!" A woman in an orange hard hat waved the people back. "Until the house is completely leveled, I want everyone behind the curb."

The woman gave the excavator operator a thumbs-up, and he started his engine. The scooper bit its big buck teeth into the porch first. The sound of breaking glass and splintering wood was terrifically loud.

"Our headquarters," Annie whispered. "My house."

The machine chomped massive bites from the front of the house, exposing the living room and staircase. A cloud of dust rose from the destruction.

"Wow, what a mess!" said someone in the crowd. "Whose house is that?"

"Nobody's now," Annie answered.

Natalie was in trouble. After marching her straight up to her bedroom, Natalie's parents commanded her to sit on the bed.

"Can you imagine how worried we were?" her mother asked. "We had no idea where you were. You could've been kidnapped or run over or who knows what!"

"I know," Natalie said. "Our plan went wrong." She looked down at her feet, which were still chilled from the cold night in the closet.

"Even if everything had gone according to your plan," said her dad, "you still would have trespassed on private property, where you could've gotten very, very hurt."

"I'm sorry. We just wanted to help Mr. and Mrs. Warsaw." Natalie pulled the covers over her head. "The only reason we went to Annie's old place was to find the comic books. They're worth a lot of money. If the Warsaws sell them, they won't have to sell their house to afford Emily's new medication."

For a few moments, all Natalie heard was her own breathing against the covers.

"Are those comic books really worth something?" her mom asked. "Enough to save the Warsaws' house?"

"Yes."

Someone sat on the bed and rested a hand on Natalie's knees. The bedsprings squeaked once more, so Natalie knew that both of her parents were sitting with her.

"Our girl," her dad said.

Her mom sighed. "Our crazy, kind girl."

After promising her parents she would never do anything so dangerous again, Natalie slept for twenty hours straight.

BALLOT

PRESIDENT
☐ TRINA
☐ PETER

VICE PRESIDENT
☐ VINCE
☐ LILA

TREASURER
☐ JOEY
☐ ROBERT

SECRETARY
☐ CLARA
☐ STEVEN
☐ NATALIE

Chapter Twenty-Two

When she woke up on Monday morning, Natalie whispered to the paint-chip lady, "It's election day." Through her lacy pink curtains, the world was bright with the first snow. Gray tree branches were dressed in fuzzy whiteness, and the ground seemed to glow. Natalie took this as a good sign.

On the bus, Trina talked about how long it took to style her hair that morning, so it would look great in the Student Council yearbook picture. Her extra-curly hair bounced every time the tires hit a pothole.

As Natalie was walking into school, Steven tapped her shoulder and said, "Hey, Secretary." He was so close, she could smell his hair gel and wintergreen gum. Another good sign.

One at a time, each grade voted in the gym, in the voting booths set up under the basketball hoop. After Natalie voted with her class, there was nothing to do but wait until the announcement during sixth period.

Natalie was in the middle of a tricky math problem when the loudspeaker crackled.

"Good afternoon, students. This is Principal Tangleton. We have finished tallying the votes, and I'm pleased to announce our new Student Council members."

From the seat behind Natalie, Missy gave one of Natalie's braids a friendly tug. After smiling at Missy, Natalie smoothed her braid back into place. And she made sure her shirt was tucked in. Tucked-in shirts looked nice in yearbook pictures.

"President: Trina George."

Doy and duh! Natalie thought cheerfully.

"Vice President: Lila Fisher. Treasurer: Robert Hall. Secretary: Steven Redding. Winners, please come to the office immediately for photos. We'll be back in a few minutes with acceptance speeches."

That's it? She lost?

Missy tugged Natalie's braid again, more gently this time, but Natalie didn't feel like turning around. The boy in the desk next to Natalie's frowned.

"You didn't win," he said with disappointment.

Natalie faked a laugh and said, "Oh, well. I don't care," which was a world away from the truth. To escape the pitying stares of her classmates, Natalie went back to her math worksheet: *Thirteen thousand times twelve . . . thirteen thousand times twelve equals me not ever running the School Store, divided by President Trina times Steven sitting next to her at Student Council meetings. The remainder divided by Natalie Wallis equals zero.* Her pencil lead snapped. The numbers on her paper swam.

At this very moment, all the winners would be milling around the office, giving each other high fives. Miss Vang would instruct everybody to line up against the wall for the photo, and Steven would be sure to stand next to Trina.

After what felt like forever, the loudspeaker came back on. "Hello, Newton Academy, this is Trina

George, your new president. I'd like to thank my campaign manager for all the support, and thank you for your votes. While I have your attention, I'd like to say that I have an audition for a new shampoo commercial this afternoon, so wish me luck!" Trina giggled, and Natalie imagined her swishing her commercial-worthy hair in a way that would make Steven fall permanently in love with her.

Natalie missed the acceptance speeches from the vice president and treasurer, but Steven's voice brought her back to earth. "Uh, Natalie Wallis? If you're listening, meet me outside the office. Thanks."

A chorus of "ooooOOOOoooo" rose from the girls in Natalie's class.

As she walked down the empty hallway, Natalie listened to her shoes echo on the wooden floor. She noticed something strange. Though she felt defeated, her footfalls sounded powerful and confident. Like the steps of a leader. Natalie had not won, and she would not run the School Store, but that didn't change the fact that she had given a great speech. She had taken charge. And nothing, not even a lost election, could take that away from her.

Outside the main office, Steven was leaning against the drinking fountain. When he saw her coming down the hall, he held his hand up in a motionless wave that almost seemed shy.

"Hey," he said.

"Hey, Steven. Congratulations."

Steven dropped his gaze to the polished floorboards. "You were supposed to win. That was the plan."

"Plans don't always go the way we plan," Natalie joked. "People voted for you, and you won. It's okay."

Steven gave her a sideways smile. "Why are you always so nice, even when you don't have to be?"

"You want me to be mean?"

"Can you imagine what Trina would've done if she lost?" Steven said. He pulled out imaginary long hair.

"She'd freak! She'd get so mad, all that makeup would melt off her face."

"Totally!" Natalie laughed. "But I thought you liked her."

"Not really," Steven said. "She already has a boyfriend from camp, and she only likes me as a friend. And between us, she's kind of a jerk." He nervously played with the drinking fountain, tapping the water on and off, on and off. "I have to ask you something."

Natalie's heart hiccupped. "Okay."

"You're the one who knows all about the School Store. I have no idea how to order supplies or how much to charge for each little thing. So I thought that maybe, we could share the position and run the School Store together."

"You mean, we'd both be secretary?"

"Yeah," Steven said. "I already checked with Tangleton, and she said it's okay. I think it would be fun. But, what do you think?"

Think? Natalie couldn't think at all. She could only feel, and what she felt was absolute joy.

"Let's do it," she said. Natalie held out her fist and Steven knocked it with his knuckles. It was the handshake of partners. Co-secretaries. Friends.

"Awesome. See ya," he said.

Later, when Natalie replayed this magical moment in her mind, she couldn't remember how she had gotten back to her classroom. But she was pretty sure she flew.

After telling her mom the good news about Student Council, Natalie raced across the snow-sugared street to Annie's. She was about to ring the doorbell when she heard a crash inside.

"I hate you!" Annie shouted.

Natalie flattened herself against the outside wall. Who was Annie shouting at? Had her mom arrived? Was Annie already letting her have it?

"You can hate me if you like. Go right ahead." It was Ms. Hatch's voice.

"You think you're my mom, but you're not. My mom doesn't have dumb rules like you."

"Annie, I understand you're angry about the TV," Ms. Hatch said. "But yelling and breaking my pottery is not going to change your punishment."

"GOD!" There was another crash.

Natalie couldn't bear eavesdropping anymore. But when an exhausted-looking Ms. Hatch opened the door, Natalie instantly regretted ringing the doorbell.

"We're having a bit of a meltdown here," Ms. Hatch said.

"I'll come back later," said Natalie.

"NO!" Annie shouted. She grabbed Natalie by the wrist and dragged her upstairs. "Come on. You can help me pack."

Chapter Twenty-Three

"Help you pack?" Natalie said. "Where are you going?"

Annie slammed her bedroom door. "I'm running away." She dumped the contents of her school backpack onto the floor. Yanking open her top dresser drawer, she took a fistful of underwear and stuffed it into the empty pack.

"Elvis, calm down. What happened?"

"Ms. Hatch is punishing me for staying out all night on Halloween even though it was by accident," said Annie. "No TV for a month. A whole month!"

"My punishment is to play board games with Ricky whenever he asks me, for a *year*," said Natalie. "I'll trade you."

"I didn't tell you the worst part yet." Annie jammed her pillow on top of the underwear and tugged the zipper closed.

"What's the worst part?"

Annie grabbed the overstuffed backpack and stormed down the stairs. Natalie ran after her, stepping over shards of broken pottery scattered on the living room floor. Ms. Hatch sat on the couch, her pale forehead resting in her hand.

"The WORST part," Annie said loudly, "is that I got another letter from my mom in the mail. But Ms. Hatch stole it. How do I know? I found the empty envelope in the recycling box. It was in my mom's handwriting!"

Ms. Hatch looked up. "You found that? So that's what this is about. I thought you were upset about not being allowed to watch TV."

"THAT, TOO!"

"Elvis, don't yell at Ms. Hatch," said Natalie.

"I'll yell at that THIEF if I want!" Annie kicked a vase off the coffee table. It hit the wall and cracked in half. "She stole my letter because she wants to keep me prisoner here. But I'm going to California to live with my mom, like it or not. *She* won't lie to me."

Ms. Hatch stood. She walked slowly over to Annie and fixed her with a fierce stare. "Listen carefully," she said. "I did get a letter from your mother yesterday. It was addressed to *me*. Since it's my letter, I chose not to share it with you yet. Just as *you* received a letter and chose not to share it with *me*. I was waiting for the right time, and that's certainly not when you're throwing things. But if you insist, you may read my letter now."

"Give it."

"You will speak to me with respect or you will not speak to me at all," said Ms. Hatch. "And if you break anything else, I will throw my television in the trash can."

"Fine." Annie sat down hard on the couch. "Gimme the letter *please*."

"I should go now," Natalie said.

"*Sit,*" Annie said in a tone Natalie didn't feel like challenging.

Ms. Hatch returned with a folded sheet of blue paper, the same color as the first letter, and handed it to Annie. As Annie read the letter, Natalie read Annie's face. It changed from hopeful to confused to utterly heartbroken. When her eyes reached the bottom of the page, Annie curled into the back of the couch and cried loud, shaking sobs.

"I was waiting for the right time," Ms. Hatch said again, her eyes filling with tears. "But I guess there is no right time."

"What does the letter say?" Natalie asked. Without turning around, Annie handed her the paper.

Dear Ms. Hatch,

I don't know you, but I owe you many thanks for taking such good care of my girl, Annie. In her letter she told me all about you. I wish I could have met you. From what Annie said, you remind me of what my mom was like.

I'm sure Annie told you I was planning a trip to come get her. I was working with some friends to collect some cash for a car and, well, things went wrong. Armed robbery is serious in California, just like everywhere else, and I'm up for ten years in jail. I was hoping to have a fresh start with Annie, but I went and messed everything up again. I meant for things to work out this time, I really did.

Annie needs a good role model, and from what Annie has said, that's you. I'm sending some papers for you to sign, if you agree to keep taking care of Annie. I'm hoping she can have a better life with you than she could ever have with me.

I'm too ashamed to tell Annie all this in a letter myself, which is why I'm writing you instead. Tell my baby I love her, and that I'm sorry.

Frances Beckett

Natalie folded the letter and set it on the coffee table. If Annie's mom was going to jail for ten years, there wasn't any more hope of her returning. By the time she got out, Annie would be grown up. Natalie's heart ached for Annie, who still lay sobbing on the couch.

"Oh, Elvis." Natalie scooted down the couch cushions, and put her hand on Annie's heaving back.

"I knew she'd do this to me again," Annie cried. "I just *knew* it." She pulled a rumpled blue envelope — the first letter — from beneath the waistband of her pants. She tossed it to the floor.

Ms. Hatch squeezed in on the other side of Annie and eased Annie's head onto her lap. "I am so sorry," she said.

"I wish I wasn't born," Annie whispered.

"Well, I don't wish that!" Ms. Hatch said. "You are my darling firefly. I love you from here to the moon and back again."

Annie looked up at Ms. Hatch. "Are you going to leave me, too?"

"No. Never." Ms. Hatch pointed at Annie's backpack on the floor. "Are you leaving *me*?"

"I guess not." Annie rested her head back on Ms. Hatch's lap. While Ms. Hatch stroked her spiky hair, Annie closed her eyes like a newborn kitten.

"Your mom sent custody papers along with her letter. It would be my great honor to adopt you, Annie Beckett, if you would adopt me," Ms. Hatch said. "You don't have to decide now. Just think about it."

"Okay." Without leaving Ms. Hatch's embrace, Annie reached for Natalie's hand. "Tell me something, Olive. Tell me something good about the world."

"I'm going to be Student Council Secretary," Natalie said. "I get to work at the School Store."

"Really? You won?" Annie's wet eyes were wide.

"Not exactly," Natalie said. "But I got one really good vote."

That night after dinner, the phone didn't ring with Annie's usual call. So Natalie called her. Ms. Hatch answered and told her to hang on a minute while she woke Annie up. There was a creaking-door sound followed by whispers.

"Hello?" Annie's voice was thick with either sleep or sadness.

"Why are you in bed so early?"

"I wanted to think about things." The bedsprings squeaked, and Natalie imagined Annie sitting up on her elbows. "You were right all along. My mom was never going to come back."

"That's not true," Natalie said. "Your mom meant to come back for you. She committed armed robbery to get money for the trip here. It didn't work out, but she wanted it to."

"I didn't think of it that way," Annie said. "Thanks, Olive."

Natalie looked out her bedroom window at the knots of squirrel nests in the trees. All the leaves had fallen, and the first snow had melted, so the nests were exposed. "I'm worried about your mom going to jail."

"Don't be. It's not the first time she's been locked up. She was in for two years for theft before I was born."

"Oh," said Natalie. "I didn't know that."

"Because I didn't tell you. I was trying to forget," Annie said. "You know that night she left me?"

"Yeah," Natalie said. "She went to the convenience store and didn't come back."

"I always had a feeling that she robbed it, and now I'm almost positive. I think she ran away so she wouldn't get caught."

"That would make sense," Natalie said.

"I wished things would work out different this time, and that my mom would change. But all along, part of me felt everything would fall apart again. You felt it, too, and I got mad at you for admitting it. I'm sorry."

"It's okay."

"It's like on *The Arthur Milligan Mysteries*," Annie said. "Sometimes, you can predict the ending even before the first commercial break. I could tell this ending would be sad."

"The ending to your mom's story might be sad, but yours doesn't have to be. Ms. Hatch can be your real grandma now, not just your foster grandma."

"She made me hot dogs tonight as a special treat."

"See how much she cares about you, and wants you to be happy?" Natalie said. "It's going to be okay."

"I know," Annie said. "But for tonight, I feel sad, and that's that."

"Do you want me to read to you?" Natalie asked.

The springs squeaked as Annie laid back on her bed. "Is it a banned book?"

"It can be."

"Then yes."

Natalie went to her bookshelf and found the copy of *Tom Sawyer* she had bought with her own money and was saving for Annie's birthday in January. At the bottom of every page, Natalie asked, "More?" and Annie grunted, "Hmm," which meant yes. When it was close to nine o'clock, Natalie asked, "More?" but there was no answer because Annie had fallen asleep.

Chapter Twenty-Four

The following Saturday, Mr. Warsaw called Natalie's parents to invite Natalie to a special lunch. Annie was invited, too. At noon on Sunday, the girls met on Annie's side of the street, wearing their winter coats, hats, and mittens. They each carried a plastic-wrapped plate.

"Don't tell me you brought zucchini bread, too," said Natalie.

"Grandma Hatch's sugar cookies," said Annie. She pointed a mittened finger at the Warsaws' front yard. "Look, the 'For Sale' sign is gone."

"Why, if it isn't the E & O Detective Agency!" Mr. Warsaw held the porch door open. "Come in. It's chilly out. Leave your shoes here. I'll take your coats. Cookies? Oh, you didn't have to bring anything," he prattled on nervously. "Go right into the dining room. Emily's waiting for you."

Mrs. Warsaw sat at the head of the dining table wearing a paper crown and a sparkly heart-shaped stone around her neck.

"Is it your birthday?" Natalie asked.

"It's a party!" she announced. "Charles gave me a Zadie necklace. There are sandwiches."

A platter of turkey sandwiches sat in the center of the cream-colored tablecloth. A bowl of soup steamed at each of the four place settings. Natalie and Annie unwrapped their treat plates and set them on the table.

"It *is* Emily's birthday today," said Mr. Warsaw, "but that's not the only reason we're celebrating. Sit down, please. How do you take your coffee?" Natalie didn't know, because she had never drunk coffee before.

Thank goodness for Annie, who said, "Take it like

Miss Dimesworth, Olive. 'Cream till it's the color of my panty hose, and hold the sugar, Sugar.'"

"Coming right up," said Mr. Warsaw. His hand trembled as he poured two cups.

"Is everything okay?" Natalie asked.

Mr. Warsaw set the coffee pot down. "Okay?" He laughed. "Everything is much better than okay, thanks to you two."

"The 'For Sale' sign is gone," Annie said.

"Yes. We took the house off the market three days ago. Those comics sold faster than a speeding bullet." He shook his head. "So much money for something that was almost lost."

"And Emily's new medicine?" Natalie asked.

"She started taking it yesterday."

"Medicine!" Mrs. Warsaw stuck out her tongue. "Yuck." She helped herself to a turkey sandwich.

"It's too early to say for sure that it's working," said Mr. Warsaw. "But I think it is. This morning, she remembered our cat's name for the first time in months."

"Sir Littlefoot!" Mrs. Warsaw whooped.

"The most we can do is hope it slows the effects of the disease." Mr. Warsaw slid the plate of sandwiches across the table. "Please. Eat."

They ate until there were no more sandwiches, and the flower pattern on the soup bowls showed. They sang "Happy Birthday," and Natalie passed around the zucchini bread her mom had made. Annie insisted that everyone have at least one of Ms. Hatch's sugar cookies, which were shaped like Thanksgiving pilgrims.

"Zadie Zeolite only eats once a week. Yet" — Mrs. Warsaw raised a bony finger — "she is stronger than the strongest man. Wanna see?"

"Did you keep some of the comic books?" Natalie asked.

"No," said Mr. Warsaw. "We couldn't afford to. But I made copies of each issue. Show them, sweet pea." Mrs. Warsaw went into the other room and returned with a purple three-ring binder. She flipped through the plastic-covered pages.

"Look at Zadie's thighs." Mrs. Warsaw held the book open. "She can kick down a steel door. And remember: only lunch, once a week."

"Don't get any ideas, darling," said Mr. Warsaw.

"Who me? No sir." She took a second pilgrim cookie and nibbled his hat. "I love to eat."

"I'm glad you can read your Zadie comics again," said Natalie.

"Not only that," Mr. Warsaw said. "We donated photocopies to the library, so everyone can read about Zadie now. And I phoned Marvin Studios in New York City, where the Zadie comics began. I told them about your detective work and they mailed me something to give you."

He passed them each a small, tissue-wrapped package. Annie tore hers open before Natalie had picked off the first piece of tape.

"Oh," Annie breathed.

Natalie finished opening her package and found the same thing that Annie had: a red leather wallet with *E & O Detective Agency* stitched on the front in silver thread. Inside was a brass badge shaped like a shield, with their code names stamped onto the metal. Annie and Natalie turned to each other and flopped their badges open at the same time.

"These are amazing," Natalie said. "Thank you."

"Thank *you*," Mr. Warsaw said. "When Emily first started talking about Zadie, I thought she was a figment of her imagination, or part of the disease. But you girls — you detectives — believed in Emily, and solved a mystery I never imagined could exist."

"We had fun doing it," Annie said. "Didn't we, Olive?"

"Yes," Natalie said. "We made some good memories."

"The memory is a funny place," Mr. Warsaw mused. "All the years I'd known her, Emily never said a word about Zadie. When the disease took hold of her mind, it seemed Zadie was all she could remember."

"Mother and her friends threw all the comic books away," Mrs. Warsaw said, clutching the purple binder to her chest. She looked frantically at the doorways. "Don't tell Mother! She'll take these from me."

"Sweetheart, your mother has passed."

Mrs. Warsaw loosened her grip on the book and her gaze grew soft. "Oh, yes. I forgot." She turned to Annie. "My mom is gone."

"Mine, too," Annie said. "But we'll be okay."

Natalie squeezed Annie's hand under the table, and Annie squeezed back.

"You girls have done so much for us," he said. "Can we do anything for you?"

"Hmm," Annie said, drumming her fingers on her chin.

Natalie gave her a hard stare. "We're just glad we could help, right, Elvis?"

"You don't happen to have a headquarters lying around, do you?" Annie asked. "Ours just got torn down."

"How about a garage?" said Mr. Warsaw. "I always park out front."

"A whole garage?" said Annie. "Get outta town."

"It's yours."

"But *only*," Mrs. Warsaw said, "if you come up to my bedroom right now."

At Mrs. Warsaw's insistence, Natalie opened the closet door and reached between two dresses. She braced herself for Mrs. Warsaw's tearful disappointment. "Wait a minute," Natalie said. "There really *is* something here!"

She parted the curtain of hanging clothes to reveal a white panel with silver hinges and a small crystal knob.

"That wasn't there before," Annie said.

Mrs. Warsaw laughed. "It was always there. Open it."

Natalie swung the panel open on its shiny hinges. Inside were eight purple binders, lined up like a miniature library. Natalie pulled one out and paged through a colored photocopy of *The Adventures of Zadie Zeolite, Volume Three*.

"See?" Mrs. Warsaw said with a smile. "I told you."

When the girls were putting on their coats to leave, Mr. Warsaw explained how he had hired a carpenter to install the closet panel in secret. "You should've seen Emily's face when she first found it!" Mr. Warsaw giggled behind his hand, like a mischievous young boy.

Chapter Twenty-Five

One snowy evening during dinner, the phone rang.

"Natalie?" her dad called from the kitchen. "It's Annie on the line."

After Annie's two standard questions — *What are you eating? Would you trade it for hot dogs?* — she asked a third: *Can you come over to my house?*

Natalie's parents said she could go for fifteen minutes after she finished her spinach lasagna, but then it was time for homework and bed. "Wear your boots," said Natalie's mom. "It's getting deep out there."

Outside, the block was a snow globe that an

unseen hand had just shaken. The falling flakes hushed all the usual noises; there was only the whisper of Natalie's boots as she waded through the powder. The world felt new and strange, and stranger still with Annie's old house gone. It was a missing tooth in a wide, white smile.

Rrrrt. Rrrrt.

Down the block, in front of the Reddings' house, someone had started shoveling.

"Steven," Natalie called to the bundled shape.

The shoveler turned and pulled off his stocking cap, revealing a curly head of hair. It was Noah. He slowly waved his cap. Natalie waved back.

"How's it going?" she said.

Noah smiled a crooked sort of smile. "All right."

Natalie gazed up and down the block, now as clean and blank as a piece of paper, and she thought about the future. The future is blank, too — an unsolvable mystery. No one knows for sure what will happen. Maybe Annie would see her mom again one day. Maybe not. But either way, Natalie was sure that

Annie would be all right. She had Ms. Hatch, she had Natalie, and most of all, she had herself.

Natalie plodded across the unplowed street and through Annie's back gate. Annie answered Natalie's knock with a shout.

"It's open!"

Annie wore a smock splattered with wet red clay. She held out her hands, slimy with clay juice. "Gimme a high five, Olive," she said.

"Ha." Natalie stamped her boots on the mat.

"Wanna see what I made?" Annie asked.

"Definitely," Natalie said, hanging up her coat. "Hi, Ms. Hatch."

"Hello!" Ms. Hatch let her potter's wheel spin to a stop. "Grab a smock."

"I can't stay long tonight," said Natalie. "But maybe tomorrow."

"Annie's learning to throw pots on the wheel," Ms. Hatch said. "The good kind of throwing."

"I wanted to glue the vases I broke, but Grandma said it's easier to make new stuff," said Annie. She did her happy dance over to the shelf of drying pottery pieces, which were waiting to be fired in the kiln. "Look!" she said. "I made all this."

On one side of Annie's shelf stood four vases of different heights. On the other side were two earthenware plates with spiraled ridges like ripples in a pond. Next to the plates sat a pair of bowls and two mugs with thick handles. All of the pieces were rough and imperfect and beautiful, just like Annie.

"The vases are for Grandma, and the dishes are for our new headquarters," said Annie, turning the cups to face Natalie. Annie had scratched *E & O* into the clay with a toothpick. "They're dry now. You can touch."

Natalie ran a careful finger over the letters. "I like it. But why didn't you write 'E & O Detective Agency'?"

"We already solved the mystery of the century," said Annie. "Maybe it's time for something new. First we were spies, then detectives, and now . . ."

"Now what?"

Annie laughed. "Good question."

Thank-Yous

Candy for everyone who read my earlier drafts and
provided all kinds of support: Lisa Watson, Mom and Dad,
Eileen Beha, Erin Anderson, Ali Hensinger, Madeleine Weiser,
Angie Vo, The Sisterhood of Second Saturday Scribes, Jane Resh
Thomas and friends, Rosanne Bane, Kristin Gehrking,
Gretchen Brant, Melissa Favero, Mary Knutson,
Melissa Kestner, and Ellie Kestner.

Joy, you don't just get candy. You also get cake.

Thanks to Kara LaReau and Jen Rees, two great editors.
You've both got my vote. Thank you, Whitney Lyle,
for drawing up a storm, and *merci* to Lauren Cecil,
copyeditor, who even caught my mistakes in French.

Kisses to Marcelo, por tudo.

And thanks to the Minnesota State Arts Board
for their generous support.